GUIDEPOSTS

## CHURCH CHOIR
# MYSTERIES™

# The Highly
# Suspicious
# Halo

### Eileen M. Berger

**Guideposts®**

CARMEL • NEW YORK 10512

www.guideposts.org

"Help Me to See Thee, Lord" was written by Eileen M. Berger.

www.guideposts.org
Series Editor: Michele Slung
Cover art by Robert Tanenbaum
Cover design by Wendy Bass
Interior design by José R. Fonfrias
Interior cat illustrations by Viqui Maggio
Typeset by Composition Technologies, Inc.
Printed in the United States of America

To VICKI, JIM, AND BILL

*Our wonderful, now-grown offspring*
*whom we enjoyed and fretted over as children,*
*worried about as adolescents and teens,*
*and admire and appreciate*
*ever more and more as adults.*

*We think of you often, and always with love,*
*and with prayers for*
*and blessings upon you,*
*and with gratitude for God's grace in granting us*
*the privilege of being your parents!*

# The
# Highly
# Suspicious
# Halo

## One

**T**HE ELDERLY MAN with the pruning shears was holding on to his aluminum walker with one hand as he stared at the overblown chrysanthemums. Grinning, he then asked his red-haired niece, Gracie Parks, to join him in the attack. "You brought your pruners with you, right?"

"I was tempted, Uncle Miltie, but didn't succumb—not this time. There are a dozen things I should be doing, but it's such a lovely day I couldn't stay inside."

"I can understand that." The eighty-year-old man moved his walker enough to allow him to snip off more of the flowers. "I've seen countless autumns when we've had frosts, *killing* frosts by now, so I'm trying to keep things blooming as long as possible."

"You're doing a great job—as always." That was no exaggeration. Her uncle, George Morgan, called "Uncle Miltie" for fifty or sixty years because people claimed that his jokes were as unfunny as those of the comedian Milton Berle, certainly did have a way with flowers!

Gracie's husband, Elmo, whom she missed terribly, even though five years had passed since he'd been killed in an accident, had not had that knack. Still, he had cheerfully always kept the lawn mowed and was willing to help her plant bulbs or move a shrub or whatever else she needed.

He had been nearly as devoted to his many responsibilities around town as he was to her. Not only had he served as Willow Bend's sanitation engineer, but also was elected mayor for several terms. Yet what he'd enjoyed most of all was acting as unofficial pastor's helper at their Eternal Hope Community Church.

The truth was that it had been Elmo's special way of drawing people to him, of supporting them—and her—that made her widowhood so hard to bear. And yet, as one of the most active citizens of Willow Bend, Indiana, Gracie herself could lay claim to only a few genuinely solitary moments.

She shook her head to bring herself back to the present, and had just started to praise Uncle Miltie further when the phone rang. He turned back toward her as she pulled her cellphone from her pocket. "Hello?"

"I'm sure glad you're there, Gracie, 'cause we do have a major problem."

This was not a call she'd looked forward to, but she tried to be upbeat. "Hi, Barb, isn't it a gorgeous day?"

There was the slightest of pauses before, "Wel-l-l, yes, it is, but I've got to talk with you about that rehearsal last night."

*Oh, dear. . . .* It wasn't that Gracie was surprised—she'd have to agree that things had not gone as well as she'd hoped. "There were some rough edges."

"'Some rough *edges*'?" Barbara Jennings' voice scooted up the scale with incredulity. "It was awful! They didn't get the notes right and the timing was beyond belief. There's no *way* we can be ready for Sunday—and in front of all those people, too!"

"Oh, Barb, we weren't that bad."

"Yes, you—yes, the choir was! We'll be the laughingstock of Willow Bend—of the whole *area*, if we go ahead with that dratted choir contest!" She drew in a loud breath. "There's no way we can fix everything that's wrong—what were we *thinking* of, putting ourselves up against Waxman Tabernacle again—and all the others in this ministerium?"

Gracie ran her left hand back through her short, curly red hair. "It *was* discouraging to have Amy unable to sing. . . ."

"It certainly would have helped, but even that wouldn't have been enough."

"It might have been. I was the one to insist she not practice with us this time. I wanted her to get completely over her laryngitis—for her not to try singing those high notes. I was afraid it might make her lose her voice entirely, like what happened last winter."

7

There was a sound from the other end, but Gracie was trying, as usual, to be a peacemaker. "I talked with her this morning, and she claims she's better—that her throat doesn't hurt as much, and the huskiness is nearly gone. And remember, Barb, Rick Harding hadn't moved here yet at this time last year. With both him and Amy, we can handle it."

The response to that positive outlook seemed more a grunt than a sigh. "I do hope so! I hardly slept a wink all night, what with fretting about this. . . ." Barb, a first-class worrier if there ever was one, went on and on, until Gracie was forced to hold the phone away from her ear as, with raised brows, she looked at her uncle.

However, by the time she hung up, Barb was in a slightly better mood. Aware of this, Uncle Miltie smiled crookedly. "Well, Gracie, I take it your worthy organist/choir director's all het up about that choir concert."

"Afraid so. But then she's 'het up' about a lot of things much of the time."

"Isn't that the truth? That bantam hen's so constantly clucking about possible troubles that she can't see past the immediate *now*."

Gracie moved closer, placing her hand on his denim-shirted arm. "Well put, Uncle Miltie, an excellent analogy. Being so busy with all her fretting, she has trouble seeing those many kernels of blessings all around her."

Her pumpkin-colored cat, Gooseberry, came strolling across the yard to rub against her leg, leading Gracie to pet him and tell him again what a fine specimen of feline grace and friendship he was.

Turning back toward her house, she declared she'd better get inside and start preparing for her Sunday school lesson. Normally she started that at the beginning of a week, yet here it was, Thursday already, and she didn't even know what the Scripture was, let alone what part of the text should be emphasized!

Gooseberry followed slowly—but knew to be quick enough so that, tail curved up over his back, he could slither through the opening just as the door was closing. Heading for his food bowl, he checked to see if Grace might have placed some special tidbit there, then padded over to where she was sitting at the kitchen table. With an effortless leap he was on the chair next to hers, and, after turning three times, curled up and went to sleep.

He gave no sign of being aware of it when Marge Lawrence, Gracie's best friend, crossed their adjoining yards, looked through the screen door and, seeing Gracie at the table, walked in. "Can you spare a few minutes?"

"Of course!" She pushed back her chair and, having kicked off her shoes, walked barefoot to turn on the heat beneath the shiny copper teapot. "How do you happen to be free this morning?"

"One of the blessings of owning my own business." She gave a satisfied chuckle as she fiddled with the jacket of an outfit Gracie hadn't seen before. "Things are sorta slow today, and I was caught up with all the paperwork, so I told Nan I was leaving for a while."

"Great!" Gracie set mugs and small plates on the table before taking pink depression-glass plates from the cupboard and placing cookies on one of them.

"Ummmm. Your famous ginger cookies!" Marge reached out her perfectly manicured hand for one of the delicacies.

"Grandma's recipe—Uncle Miltie's mother's. I've always liked them, and *he* practically inhales them."

"Probably brings back a host of memories for him."

"For me, as well." Gracie nodded. "I didn't get around to making these very often after Arlen left for college, then took that job in New York." She wished that her son and his family would get home more often. "Then, after Elmo died, there seemed little reason to make them—until Uncle Miltie came to live with me."

The teakettle was giving its familiar little hum signaling that the water was ready, so she brought her assortment of tea bags in the ironstone sugar bowl. Marge checked them all before choosing the green-tea-with-mango she'd looked at first.

Gracie still preferred plain orange pekoe. She opened one of these packets and waited for her friend to let her know if there was some special reason for this visit. She could only hope, after Barb's agitated call, that it would have nothing to do with the competition coming up in just three more days. Marge was a second soprano which, in their choir, meant she'd sometimes sing with the sopranos and sometimes with the altos; she, also, had been present for last night's rehearsal.

Instead, they discussed instead the beauty of the season, commenting on several church members who were in the hospital or recuperating at home, and praising Uncle Miltie's care of Gracie's flowers and the advice he'd given Marge about hers.

It was only as she was getting ready to leave, after a second cup of tea and sixth cookie, that Marge mentioned choir practice. "Personally, I thought things went fairly well. Sure, it would have been better if Amy could have sung with us— but I appreciate the fact that she even *came*, which was more than most of us would have done with such a sore throat."

She straightened the little jacket as she got to her feet and headed for the door. ". . . Especially since she already knows by heart all the lead-in's and stuff."

"Yes, she does. And I encouraged her to not strain her voice; we can't have her unable to sing with us on Sunday."

"Yeah. Let's keep praying that her laryngitis will be completely gone by then. . . ."

Gracie was putting away her books when Uncle Miltie came in the back door and laid three perfect long-stemmed roses on the table. She picked up a deep, almost-maroon one to hold close to her nose. "Want me to get a vase for these?"

"No, I'll find something." He returned from the pantry with a tall glass vase and went to fill it at the kitchen sink before bringing it to the table and inserting the blooms. It was amazing how well he managed with his wheel-fronted walker.

She cocked her head thoughtfully. "Would you mind if I were to give these away? I'd planned to go see Joe and Anna Searfoss this afternoon. . . ."

"We've got lots more, just as pretty, still on the bushes out there," he said. Then he started back to the small, off-the-kitchen room. "I'm getting something else to take them in— so they needn't worry about sending this back."

For lunch, she made up twice as much tuna salad as they'd eat. The extra would go into her basket, along with the flowers and some cookies. She was pleased when, at the last moment, he decided to join her. It had been two years since her uncle had come from Ohio to Willow Bend, Indiana, with the understanding that he'd stay only through the winter. Thus, at first, he'd made no effort to put down roots.

Aunt Doris, his wife of fifty-six years, had recently died, and he was insisting he *would* not "butt in on his kids." But his osteoarthritis had become worse and he was having enough trouble getting around that he seriously considered selling his home and entering a senior-citizen complex.

That's when Gracie, inviting him to visit for several months, put the bed and dresser in what had been Elmo's office, off the living room. This arrangement had worked out very well, since the downstairs bathroom was the one with the walk-in shower.

His physical condition, however, began to improve, and each year saw him participating more and more in the life of the community and of the church. He even volunteered to read to kids in the local library, and sometimes drove for the Meals on Wheels deliveries, with Gracie or one of his friends doing the actual carrying-in of the food.

As they pulled away in her trusty ten-year-old Cadillac— affectionately known as Fannie May—on their way to visit their friends, Gracie took in her two-story clapboard house with the huge rhododendron bushes in the front. She couldn't help admiring the flower beds that lay not only close to the house and garage but also along the post-and-rail fences bordering both streets.

With the exception of the years he spent overseas during World War II, Joe Searfoss had been on one or another board ever since the Eternal Hope Community Church was founded in 1945—on the very day that the war ended! Anna, too, had served in many capacities, though she'd gradually relinquished responsibilities as her sight became more limited, and her over-forty-years' battle with diabetes continued to give her constant pain, due to nerve damage.

They weren't always able to go to church, so Gracie was pleased to hear Anna say, "I'm looking forward to being there for the contest on Sunday. I think our choir has a good chance to win, don't you?"

"We're doing our best, Anna. You may have heard that

Amy's got laryngitis, but we're hoping she'll be in full voice by then."

"Isn't she a sweet little thing?" The older woman's voice and face revealed her affection for the young singer. "I look forward to her solos, and often make out her voice when you sing those anthems.

"And isn't it nice that Sunday's choir-meet will be held in Waxmire Tabernacle?"

Gracie herself had been concerned that the host church would be given an advantage. She hesitated just long enough for Anna to explain, "It's not only handicap-accessible, but its pews are farther apart, so it's easier to get in with a walker—not like in our over-a-hundred-year-old structure we took over when the Presbyterians moved to their new one."

Uncle Miltie agreed. "That narrow spacing bothered me, too, at first. I finally learned how to go in sideways without tripping myself—or incapacitating someone else."

"I'm spoiled, you see." Anna smiled. "I guess I should use my walker more at home, so I'd get more used to it—but I know where everything is, and I'm usually in reach of counters, or doorways, or furniture. . . ."

"Hey, I wouldn't use *mine* if I didn't need to," Uncle Miltie reassured her. "I can stand for a while, like when pruning bushes or something, but I keep my security blanket nearby—my walker's always ready to get around with."

They talked about the eight area choirs that had signed on—especially Eternal Hope's, much smaller than the one from Waxmire, yet larger than several of the others. There was a crooked grin on Joe's face when he commented, "Way back in high school, the actual dress rehearsal for any production, whether a skit or band concert or drama, always seemed to show us at our very worst despite however many weeks or months we'd worked on it.

"None of us ever actually wanted to believe the old theater adage about the worse the final practice, the better the opening-night would be—but you know what? It *did* seem to hold true."

"Then we've nothing at all to worry about, Joe. We're a shoo-in!" Gracie sagged down in feigned relief as the others laughed. "I'm gonna hold on to that—but, in the meantime, I'll feel better if we can work in just one more rehearsal, perhaps tomorrow evening. . . ."

With that thought uppermost in her mind, she took her uncle home before going on to stop at a small, cream-colored, aluminum-sided house near the end of Main Street. There she found Barb even more upset, if possible, and convinced that their choir was going to "bomb."

"Uncle Miltie and I stopped at Joe and Anna's a little while ago," Gracie told her, "and Joe reminded us of the old adage about 'good rehearsal, poor production. Poor rehearsal, *good* show.'"

"If only that were true—but it's *not*, and you know it!" The other woman was distraught. "We should just drop out."

Gracie, having expected Barb's pessimism, now made a

counterproposal, "Or what would you think of calling one more rehearsal?"

"It's a waste of time, Gracie, *that's* what I think!" She ran her hand back through her already tousled salt-and-pepper hair. "You were there—you know we had all kinds of problems. And some of the music is just too convoluted, especially that required one, *Hallelujah, Save Us, Lord*. I'm already kept much too busy to work in any more special directing for the contest."

She frowned. "Besides, some of our members still have no sense of counting out the beat, or where to come in when the accompaniment's different from their notes. . . ."

Gracie couldn't deny any of that, but still: "Maybe if we went over it a couple more times—not necessarily the whole thing, you know, just working on problem areas . . . ?"

"Oh, Gracie!" Barb sighed very slowly and deliberately. "Honestly, I wouldn't even know where to begin."

"But—the thing is, it's already in the paper—Rocky gave us such wonderful coverage, far more than he had to—even sending the photographer to take those pictures of each of the choirs. I—I'd really hate not to follow through." Rocky Gravino was more than just *The Mason County Gazette's* editor-in-chief, he was a cherished friend of Gracie's, someone she could turn to with problems—and with whom she could also share joys.

"But. . . ."

She had to be firm with Barb. "Remember that the name of

16

our church is already on the printed program—and we're in the sixth position, which, in fact, I think is a good place to be. . . ."

"It's—too much pressure, Gracie. I can't *handle* this—I really can't!" That was getting closer to the truth.

"Would you consider it if I were to assist with the directing?" How had that slipped out? Gracie had had no intention of making such an offer, but now it was too late to wonder about the wisdom of getting so involved.

"Wel-l-l, that *might* help. . . ."

Barb had started to look somewhat more cheerful, and Gracie decided that a bit of flattery still might be advisable. "I'd be starting at square one—I'd need an *awful* lot of help. . . ."

Barb crossed the room to bring two pieces of music from her baby grand. "I've been trying and trying to make it simpler to get them started at the exact moment, but nothing so far has worked consistently."

"So how about sitting here on the sofa with me, and we'll see if we can maybe figure out some way to get them coming in together better."

It wasn't an easy task—but Gracie hadn't expected it to be. They began with the song each choir was required to sing, the one with which Eternal Hope's choir had experienced trouble right from the start.

She asked to see the rules for the contest, and checked them carefully. "Well, it appears to be the same as for other years, doesn't it? The choir's size is immaterial, and the words and melody of any music must be retained. But just about anything else—rhythm, beat, use of solo or duet or multi-part sections, can be altered. . . ."

She struggled to keep the smile from her face as she again read the hymn's name: *Hallelujah, Save Us, Lord*. Rick Harding had earned a glare from Barb when he suggested wryly at the last practice, "There can't be a more apt request, considering what we're doing to this music tonight!"

She couldn't now risk making such a joke but, treating Barb as her mentor, asked questions and tried to be constructive when it came to putting advice into practice. She was also grateful that their headstrong organist didn't seem to be feeling threatened, for after working on the first selection to their satisfaction, Barb suggested that Gracie also be the one to lead their "anthem-of-choice."

The decision-making for this piece had been difficult, as they hadn't wanted something too simple or too familiar, like a variation on *Amazing Grace*—nor did they want a piece no one would recognize or enjoy. They finally settled upon one Marge suggested, saying she'd heard *Help Me to See Thee, Lord* sung as a solo while visiting her elderly mother the year before.

"I especially like the words and the *feel* of this one," Barb remarked now.

"Me, too. It's not *deep* or anything, but it's good to be

reminded that no matter what happens, God still loves us. Even when things don't go the way we think is best, He's there—though we sometimes have to make a conscious effort to look for Him."

"I confess this has been one of those times when I sure haven't been feeling His presence." Barb shifted position. "I guess I should have been working harder at *seeing* God in all of this."

Up until now, almost all of it had been sung in four-part harmony, but today they played around with various possibilities for different portions. Perhaps the men alone there in the middle section, with several brief duets and solos? The women could then take care of the part immediately prior to the closing, when everyone would sing softly, repeating the title words twice. Then Amy would take it one more time, alone.

They began calling the choir members, Gracie using her cell phone to speed the process. They'd anticipated groans from one and all at the thought of scheduling an emergency, unexpected rehearsal tomorrow night, Friday, at 7:00. However, after the very first call, they obligingly changed the time to 5:30, since Amy told them about a 7:30 program at the high school to which several choir members, including herself, would be going.

"That should be fine," Gracie assured her. "And I'll tell you what, I'll bring meat, cheese, and bread for sandwiches, and two kinds of soup for anyone getting there by 5 o'clock or a little later. If we've already started rehearsing before some arrive, they can eat after practice."

Almost unbelievably, every single choir member told them he or she could be there for all or most of the practice! "Talk about the Lord providing!" Gracie exclaimed, tucking her handy little phone back in her pocket and heading for the door.

She started for home, but then, changing her mind, she pulled up instead in front of the *Gazette* office. Going inside, she could see Rocky busily working at his big desk, which took up almost a third of the glassed-in area. However, in order to make her way back there, she first had to stop and exchange greetings with several other friends on the staff, and by then he'd seen her.

"Welcome!" He came around the desk to hold both of her hands in his for a moment before seating her in one of the two straight chairs. He took the other, instead of going back to his own. "To what do I owe the pleasure of this visit?"

She gave a pretend-frown. "Can't I just drop in to say *hello*?"

"Any time you choose, Gracie. You know you're always welcome." He gave her a slow, warm smile. "Unfortunately, you don't take advantage of that opportunity very often. Ergo, I suspect you have something on your mind."

"Transparent as a fresh-cleaned window, that's what I am."

"And I like freshly cleaned windows, even though," indicating the big ones between him and the rest of the staff, "some make my life an open book."

"In a town the size of Willow Bend, *most* people's lives seem to be that way."

"True. Very true," he agreed. "But I suspect you came for a totally different reason other than discussing glass and gossip. Is everything okay with you?"

"I—hope so. I guess I'm not too bright, however, or I wouldn't have volunteered this morning to take over for Barb at the competition on Sunday."

"So they're sending in the relief pitcher," he teased. "I'll look forward to that."

"Just so you—and others—aren't disappointed." She was beginning to wish she had not made that impulsive offer.

Rocky was about her age, but stockier, and four or five inches taller than her five-four. "Knowing you, Gracie, I have no doubts that you'll do your very best, and so will everyone else." He shrugged. "So how could I be disappointed?"

"Thanks, Rocky. That's what I needed to hear today—some sane person encouraging us just to do the best we can."

"Sounds like you've been having a rough time."

"Well, we haven't done an especially good job on one number all along—and did even worse on both of them at last night's practice. Barb even got upset enough to try to convince some of us that the wisest course was to walk away from Sunday's contest. You know how she is, but somehow that didn't seem like the right thing to do."

"So—I'm assuming that's when you made your generous offer." He lifted his eyebrow quizzically.

"It was obviously a moment of insanity."

They laughed together, but she pretended to take offense. "I don't expect us to do *that* poorly."

"I don't expect you to do poorly at all—and you know it Plus, you know that wasn't why I was laughing."

They'd been friends for years, ever since he arrived from Philadelphia to take over this eighty-year-old paper. Elmo had met him when he'd been just considering the purchase, and Rocky often reminded her that his first meal in Indiana had been eaten in their home.

It felt good to sit here, talking comfortably. However, before long she was obliged to say, "I must get home—and you need to be freed so you can do your writing and editing and assigning and whatever else you do."

She was already at the door when she turned to ask, "You're coming to hear us Sunday? To hear all of us?"

"I wouldn't miss it. And I'm bringing Ben Tomlinson, our ace shutterbug, to capture what I hope will be a special triumph!" He had walked to the door with her. "I'm going to be rooting for you, my friend."

"Is an editor allowed to be partial to one choir over another?"

"I *am* human, dear girl, even though you may not have noticed. And there could be no rules as to my having feelings and interests, so yes, I may root for my friends."

"I'm glad." A glance out into the editorial department made her realize that some of the employees had been watching. "There are people wondering what's going on in here."

"So be it."

"Thanks for letting me steal your time, Rocky. I'm supposed to be such a great *coper*, but I'm not always. So I came to see you, someone not directly related to the choir, to make me think about other things, and yet I was the one to bring up the topic! Ah, the inconsistencies of being a woman."

His hand rested for the briefest of moments against the small of her back. "Ah, the inconsistencies of being a member of the human race. . . ."

# Two

GRACIE WENT OUT for her usual brisk walk the next morning, Gooseberry accompanying her. But she didn't talk to him much, as she often did when using him as her sounding board, for she had a book-on-tape she'd borrowed from the library. It wasn't that she was bored, for she loved nature any time of the year, but sometimes she just felt like doing things a bit differently.

Her niece, Carter Stephens, had recommended this book to her. "You'll love it, Aunt Gracie. It takes place in a town remarkably similar to Willow Bend—it even has as many zany characters per block!"

"Zany characters?" Gracie repeated in mock dismay. "You think we have zany characters?"

Carter laughed. "How could I ever have entertained such a thought?"

"Present company excluded?"

Her eyes were sparkling. "But of course. How could you possibly think otherwise . . . ?"

Gracie adored her niece, but with her working as hard as she did in Chicago, Carter didn't get to visit very often. She reminded Gracie that it was equally distant in whichever direction one traveled, and made clear that she'd love to take her aunt around the city, to the museum and the zoo and whatever else suited her fancy.

But Gracie seldom drove up there anymore, for it wasn't the same without Elmo. When he was still living they'd make it a special weekend or more, going to the Pump Room for their wedding anniversary or getting tickets for a concert or a play.

Maybe she *should* go, however—perhaps for Christmas. But that was an almost-*less*-than-fleeting thought, for Christmas was one of the busiest seasons in the church and community. And since Uncle Miltie had been with her, there was someone else to consider. Not to mention Gooseberry.

Where *was* that cat? He could disappear faster than. . . . Oh, there he was, crouched down in checkmate-position in front of a big German shepherd. The dog was straining on its leash, nose less than a foot from Gooseberry's, apparently having no idea what a force he'd have to reckon with should the cat decide to slash out with its long, sharp claws.

Gracie hurried toward the face-off. A slender young woman—a girl, actually, maybe sixteen years old—was tugging with all her might and yelling for the dog to back off.

He, however, employing canine selective-hearing, chose to ignore the panicky human voice.

"Come on, Gooseberry," Gracie urged soothingly. "Let's go back home."

He kept his eyes on the dog, making no move to obey—which she had to admit was wise under the circumstances. "Make sure you hold your dog," Gracie told the girl as she reached down, placed her hands around the cat's muscular body and picked him up. As Gooseberry hissed his contempt of the other animal, the dog's attempted leap ended in his crashing back down on the sidewalk, then scrambling back to his feet, yelping the entire time.

"I'm very sorry," the girl apologized, now with tight hold of the collar. "I'm supposed to be dog sitting for the Berkmeyers this weekend, and they told me to take Fritz for walks—that he listens well. . . !"

"This is the first time you've tried it?" Gracie was still holding Gooseberry in her arms. "They may think he does obey, whereas it's only the *master's* voice he recognizes as an authority—it's only the master he obeys."

"I assumed when they said he listens, that he *would*."

"Well, no harm was done."

"And there won't be any, either," she stated firmly. "Once I get him back in his run, he's staying there!"

They walked together until the dog and his sitter turned off on their side street. Gracie then finished her three-mile circuit, trying harder now to keep Gooseberry in sight at all times.

She wasn't listening to the tape anymore, however, too busy thinking of what she'd just said to the girl. *Help me, too, Lord, to listen to Your voice, my Master's voice. Sometimes I don't seem to recognize it as well as I should.*

۶

One good thing about preparing to eat at her own church tonight was that she could use the plates and silverware already there, rather than buying disposable items. As spur-of-the-moment as it was, this rehearsal still counted, to Gracie, as a church function!

She'd checked her supply of vegetables when getting the large chuck roast from the chest freezer and had put the meat in the slow-cooker before she and Gooseberry went for their walk. It was safe to leave that simmering until mid-afternoon, when she'd cut up the meat, removing all fat or gristle. And since she had a good supply of fresh carrots, potatoes, and onions, these vegetable-soup makings could be thrown together later.

Gracie also prepared chili, using ground turkey instead of hamburger, as several choir members were currently shunning red meat. Since she was using dried kidney beans, it would take very slow cooking in order to blend the full flavor of the seasonings with all the other ingredients. So that, too, she prepared before lunch.

It seemed that everything she did wound up being interrupted by phone calls. Sometimes this could be annoying, yet she realized that many people, particularly older ones, were lonely and felt the need to make contact with someone. She told herself she should feel grateful to be able to help in this way—but sometimes that was hard, when she was aware of how much she had to get done.

One call was from Anna Searfoss, telling how much they'd enjoyed the food Gracie had brought. "And it was so good to talk with you! Joe and I realize how busy you are, Gracie, and I know I shouldn't be bothering you, but it's just not that easy for me to talk with people now that I can't see their faces—to know how they're reacting to whatever I'm saying."

"That—would be a problem." Gracie tried to imagine just how different that would be, how difficult.

"Well, at least it's not too bad at church, anymore. People there understand how bad my vision is—but at a store, or elsewhere, they often just back away, as though blindness is catching, or something."

"Maybe they're just trying to make it easier for you, Anna. Just trying to get out of your way."

"Oh, yes, for *some* that could be the case, but not for most." She then gave what sounded like a little chuckle. Yet Gracie recognized it wasn't entirely humor she was expressing when adding, "And many talk louder, as though if I don't see well, I probably don't *hear* well, either. . . ."

Later in the afternoon, shortly before she left for church

with the food, the voice she heard on the other end when she picked up the phone sounded very young. "Hi, Miss Gracie. This is Patsy. I just wondered how Gooseberry's doing?"

*Ah, Patsy Clayton, from Vacation Bible School last June.* "Hello, Patsy. Gooseberry's doing very well, thank you, and he and I want to know how *you* are."

"Pretty good—now. The doctor operated on my leg again, and it doesn't hurt so much as it did."

"Is there a cast on it?"

"Um-hmmm, but the doctor says he's going to take it off next week if everything's okay."

"Are you using crutches?"

"Sometimes. Mostly my walker. And Mrs. Johnson comes to my house two times each week, so I'm keeping up at school even if I can't go to classes. But I'll sure be glad to get back again after Thanksgiving. . . ."

"I'm sure you will, Patsy." This child, a gentle fourth-grader, had never called before, and Gracie couldn't help wondering what had led up to it now.

"You and Gooseberry went past my house today, but you were going so fast I couldn't get to the door to call to you. I thought maybe if—well it would be nice if you could stop sometime. I'd like to pet your cat again."

She'd almost forgotten having taken Gooseberry to Vacation Bible School one day. Patsy had been very quiet, almost unresponsive during the first session, but had immediately bonded with the cat, holding him on her lap and stroking him and telling him how wonderful he was. "I'm not sure where you live, Patsy."

"Right next to Amy. She's on the corner, and I'm right next to her house. That's how I went to your church for Vacation Bible School—she brought me."

"That's nice, dear. And does Amy bring you to Sunday school, too?" If so, Gracie hadn't seen her.

"No, but she asked me. Maybe after the cast comes off."

"I'll look for you there, dear." She glanced up at the clock. Now she'd really have to hurry to get to the church in time to get everything done. She closed the conversation with, "Gooseberry and I will stop at your house soon, I promise."

Unexpectedly, it was times like this that Uncle Miltie sometimes chose to feel sorry for himself. "If only I could help you carry out all that food!" he grumbled. "It's *awful* that you have to make trip after trip to the car, while I sit here like a lump!"

"You're a lovable lump," she teased lightheartedly. "And I'm glad you're here."

He tried to ignore that with, "I came to spend one winter, as you remember—and look at me! Talk about overstaying one's welcome!"

She was crossing the kitchen with the large electric slow-cooker filled with hot vegetable soup. "If *you* aren't happy with the arrangement, Uncle Miltie, all you have to do is say so. As for me, you continue to be a blessing." And she went out, letting the screen door bang shut behind her for emphasis.

She'd left a container of chili for his supper and would

have put out an entire meal had she not been so sensitive to his determination to "be no more trouble than absolutely necessary." She wondered what had put him in that mood this time, though she realized from experience it would soon pass.

She could appreciate how difficult it had to be for such a previously active person to be unable to do all those things he'd formerly done, and suspected she'd be worse than Uncle Miltie should she be restricted that much.

He had been a successful builder who could do just about anything from masonry to roofing, from drywalls to driveways. And now, even with his walker, he'd quietly made many repairs to her house and garage, many of them things she'd not even recognized as needing attention.

Even more important was just having him here. After being married to and living with her beloved Elmo all those years, her home had become incredibly quiet, unbelievably *empty* with just her and Gooseberry in it.

She was the first to arrive, as she'd hoped to be. Of course it would have been nice to have someone there to help carry, but she was used to it. First, she took in the cold sandwich and salad makings, then the hot soups and, after that, everything else. Gracie had always enjoyed cooking, and during these last years had been called upon more and more to cater luncheons, dinners, brunches, and picnics.

She didn't have to, though, because even if she wasn't

wealthy, Elmo had enough insurance, in addition to stocks and bonds, to let her live comfortably. But she *liked* preparing meals and planning parties.

She'd certainly had enough practice behind the scenes here at the church, for festive occasions, and at all of Arlen's Boy Scout meetings, church camps and school activities she used to be so involved with!

Back in the early sixties, when their church bought this aging wooden building, there had been only the big sanctuary, a small chapel room and bathroom, plus the space beneath it. This consisted of a small kitchen and furnace room, and a large room split into classrooms by homemade dividers, which could be rolled back against the wall for dinners or wedding receptions or meals following a funeral.

But when the huge addition was added about thirty years ago, they finally gained adequate classrooms on both floors, as well as the large Family Activity Center. *This* time the women, the ones who'd be using it the most, got in on the planning and design of the first-floor kitchen. What a blessing that was, and how Gracie appreciated it! Although it wasn't terribly large, everything was now so well organized that it was a joy to work in.

Gracie was grateful that they'd retained the old flow-green glass in the sanctuary windows, which contrasted beautifully with the white vinyl siding that unified the old and new portions of the building.

Used to working alone, she buzzed around getting the jugs of cider in the refrigerator, the coffee perking, hot water ready for tea, and everything laid out and ready by the time the first singers arrived. It took only minutes for them to move three long tables end-to-end and get chairs in place so that as others arrived they could dish up their soup, make a sandwich, and find a seat.

Gracie was amazed and grateful that even Barb seemed in good spirits, and that there was so much relaxed joking and having fun. Amy arrived too late to eat before practice, but her voice seemed much better. Both Gracie and Barb, having every reason to believe she'd do her usual good job on Sunday, cautioned her not to strain for those very high notes tonight.

They gave a three-minute-warning just before 5:30. After this, the choir entered the sanctuary, with latecomers knowing they could eat afterward. Gracie wanted all sixteen of them first to get in the order in which they'd be singing on Sunday afternoon. Having checked and found there'd be three levels of wide risers placed on Waxmire's platform, she had them practice the procession so everything would go smoothly. By the third try, everyone successfully crossed the platform to end up in proper configuration.

For the sake of the few later in arriving, Barb explained again that Gracie would be taking over the directing for tonight and on Sunday, as well. There were a few raised eyebrows but no negative comments—after all, she'd led them for several cantatas and when Barb was on vacation, and they knew her capabilities.

They began with the required number, the *Hallelujah* one, but this time—with Gracie stressing that she and Barb had together made the changes—several of the most difficult passages for the entire choir were marked for solos and two-part harmony.

Don Delano, the thirty-year-old chemistry teacher, one of their baritones, asked if that meant they were still observing the rules. "We won't be disqualified or penalized if we do this, will we?"

Barb was the one to reassure him, "We've gone over everything, and there's nothing in the information we received that says we can't make these changes."

Estelle Livett, overly conscious of being the only member of this choir who'd ever studied under a *real* singing teacher (albeit twenty-some years previously) now volunteered to take Amy's place in the solo—because of the girl's laryngitis, of course, to help save her voice.

Gracie glanced at Amy to see her reaction, and found the teenager was smiling. "I appreciate your offering, Estelle," Amy told her, "but I really think I'll be okay."

Realizing that all of them were aware that Estelle's "operatic" tones and pretentious manner would do nothing to help them win, Gracie courteously thanked her for making the offer. She managed to get through the difficult moment by saying they'd have to wait to see how Amy got along before making additional changes—and struggled to keep a straight face when Marybeth Bower, another soprano, winked at her.

Don and Amy were asked to take the first short duet, about a third of the way through the number. Rick Harding, the only African American in the choir—although there were two other black families in the congregation besides him, his wife, and two-year-old daughter—was given the eleven-bar tenor solo near the middle. Amy then would begin the one near the end, with Rick joining her.

As the practice got underway at last, first with just the chosen ones going over their parts and then the whole choir running through *Hallelujah, Save Us, Lord* from beginning to end, Gracie felt relief. Not unexpectedly, there were some rough sections, but everyone worked at going back over the difficult bits again. After singing through it one final time in its entirety, they all agreed it was excellent.

And then it was time to start their second number, the one everyone liked best, *Help Us to See Thee, Lord*. Here, too, modifications were made and several solo and duet parts given out. They started out very well:

> "I know that You are with me,
>    I know You really care,
> But sometimes it is hard, God,
>    To feel You with me there.
>
> "When days and nights are dreary,
>    Or. . . ."

As their voices joined together, with Amy well into her solo part, suddenly, unaccountably, she went *way* off pitch!

The sound of it was so unusual that Gracie stared in amazement. She became even more concerned when she realized the girl was standing there with her hand pressed to her head, a look of distress, then fear, taking over her expression. Gracie dropped her music and raced up the steps. Amy's eyes had rolled upward unseeingly and her knees seemed unable to support her as she started to crumple downward. "Grab her, Rick! Amy's falling!"

Don helped Rick ease her down upon the maroon carpet. Murmurs of alarm rose agitatedly around her. What happened? What's wrong? Is she going to be all right?

But, at that tense moment, answers were in short supply.

Gracie handed Don her cell phone with, "Call 911!" and was down on her knees on one side of the unconscious Amy, prepared to help Rick, a volunteer EMT with the Willow Bend Volunteer Fire Company. "I've taken Red Cross courses, Rick, but never had to use them. Tell me what to do, and I'll try my best."

She was dimly aware of Pastor Paul Meyer arriving and of hearing someone filling him in about what happened, but she was much too busy even to look around. It seemed forever before the ambulance got there, and only then was Gracie able to get to her feet, letting a better-trained professional take over.

Suddenly she realized she herself was shaking and Marge was putting her arms around her, while Lester Twomley, one of the tenors, had come over to help lead her to the front pew. "Lean forward," he urged. "Put your head down."

She was suddenly thoroughly annoyed with herself. How could she, Gracie, be acting like some stupid little Victorian female who collapsed at the least upset? "I'm fine," she assured them, sitting bolt upright. "I've never fainted in my life, and I'm not about to!"

"Glad to hear that, Gracie." Lester was smiling down at her. "You took over like a pro when you were needed, and I'm proud of you."

"Hmmph!" She wasn't so proud of herself right then, and forced herself to get up on her feet. She wasn't too prideful, however, to murmur, "Thanks, Don," as his arm went around her waist, and they walked over to where Amy was being lifted onto the gurney to be wheeled to the ambulance.

Rick left with them, so someone familiar might be with her on the way to the hospital. Looking around, Paul suggested, "How about you folks going on with your practice? I'm following the ambulance to Keefer Memorial—and will start the prayer chain as soon as I get there."

"You'll call us, too, won't you?"

"Of course, Gracie." He patted her shoulder. "Just as soon as I learn anything."

He was going out the door when she called after him, "Are you going to notify Amy's parents, or should I?"

"I'd appreciate your taking care of that. They'll have questions, of course, and I just got here."

She nodded and, taking the cell phone from her pocket, made the call. It was awkward not being able to tell Linda and Roy any more than that Amy had had some sort of attack or seizure and passed out. Yes, the ambulance was on its way to Keefer.

She also told them who was manning the ambulance and that Pastor Meyer had followed it and would soon be starting the prayer chain.

Hanging up, she informed the anxious choir members that Amy's parents were leaving immediately for the hospital. "And before we start singing again, I think we should pray for Amy and her family and all those working with her. . . ."

They made a circle, holding hands as they prayed, then went back to their *Help Me . . .* anthem. It seemed to go well, especially considering the frightening interruption, and Gracie even made a few additional changes. Always in the back of her mind was the need for constant attention to each individual voice, especially the tenors.

She already knew that Rick had a remarkably wide range, but Lester and Don did beautifully this time, also, so she asked them to please stay after the others were excused. Should Amy not be able to sing with them Sunday, which seemed likely, she explained that Lester would have to be ready to take her place in the required numbers, while Don and Rick would handle that part for *Help Me to See Thee, Lord.*

They went over these sections several more times, and through the entire program twice before making arrangements to come early on Sunday morning to practice both anthems in their entirety.

Still having heard nothing from the hospital, Gracie remembered to call Uncle Miltie to tell him not to worry if she got home very late since she wanted to stop and check on Amy's condition and talk to her parents.

Having learned that Amy was in the Intensive Care Unit, Gracie went directly to the ICU waiting room. Putting her arms around Linda Cantrell, who was sitting on the three-cushioned couch, crying, she learned that the parents and pastor had heard nothing more than that Amy was considered to be in critical condition.

Was there any way to make sense of it? Could it have been something she'd eaten? She'd been a little later than usual coming home from school, but had told her mother only that she'd been hanging out with friends. No, she'd not mentioned them by name.

She'd then sat at the kitchen table, as she often did, to finish her calculus assignment, but refused a cookie or an apple, which she'd normally have eaten while doing this. Linda said she *should* eat something, but Amy told her she'd wait until getting to the church. She did, however, have a diet soda— which led to her father's comment that she certainly didn't have to watch her weight, as thin as she was!

Amy had mentioned the possibility of meeting someone

after practice, and maybe going to a movie. No, she hadn't said which friend that was, but her mother assumed it was Francine Barton, with whom she frequently went to youth activities at the church or for a pizza or to the mall.

This reminded Linda to call Francine to let her know what had happened. The girl was a bit hysterical at first, then informed Amy's mother that she intended to come to the hospital right away.

The teen was just entering the waiting room as Dr. Floyd Jennings came through the door from the Intensive Care Unit to talk with them. Amy was still unconscious. The test results weren't in, but her vital signs were improving. He also asked a number of questions, particularly as to what she'd eaten and drunk. Then he said it would be fine for her parents and the pastor to go in to see her for a few minutes.

Gracie used this opportunity to talk with Francine. "We're always together during our last class of the day," she was told, "and, though there are a couple of other students between us, we're in the same homeroom.

"But we didn't walk home together like we often do, my house being just a block before hers. Today Amy said she had to make a stop on the way home."

"Do you know what this stop was?"

Francine shook her head, frowning. "Come to think of it, maybe she said she had to meet someone. I'm not sure about that, but I *do* know she seemed okay, and was looking forward to the practice at the church and eating there."

"Can you remember anything else you talked about?"

"Well, some stuff about the all-day Youth Fellowship project eight days from now. We've volunteered to do interior painting at the new Habitat for Humanity house, since that's almost ready for the people to move in. And I asked if tonight's singing could hurt her throat—but Amy insisted it was already much better.

"She was really looking forward to singing this Sunday!"

No, there had been no mention of feeling ill or of any other problem. Amy had been very much herself—if anything, she was *more* cheerful and "up," probably because of the upcoming concert.

But Amy's not having mentioned the possibility of going to a movie following the rehearsal did seem strange to Francine, since they usually told each other everything.

The Cantrells were wiping their eyes when they returned to report that their daughter hadn't responded to their presence. Pastor Paul, looking very serious, borrowed Gracie's phone to call the church to inform the chairman of their diaconate board to go ahead with the scheduled meeting, since he felt he should stay with the Cantrells at the hospital.

Amy's mother tried to release him with, "Really, Pastor, it's all right for you to leave. . . ."

Gracie had decided that she, too, should remain with Amy's parents. However, she did think to inquire if there was anything Paul had planned to bring to the meeting in addition to what was already on the agenda—or if he'd planned to handle any particular matters in a certain way. Learning that this was the case, she asked him to come out in the hall with her, where they discussed her attending as his emissary. After all, his presence was needed here more than hers was.

She was a little surprised when arriving at the church to find the meeting hardly begun. Instead, they had spent time in prayer for Amy and her family.

"And not only our own prayer chain has been activated, but that of the other four Willow Bend churches, which have chains like ours," Don told her. "So if you have anything additional to share about Amy's condition, we'll get that out, too."

She shook her head. "No, nothing more as of now. I just wish there were."

They finally got the business of the evening attended to, but it took longer than usual since the group kept speculating about possible causes for Amy's blackout, and also about her prognosis. Gracie confessed, "I've been going over what happened ever since I saw her start to fall. It was so *sudden*! So unexpected! It's true she had laryngitis several days ago, but this is—I don't know—something else altogether. It's . . . suspicious even."

Rick shook his head reprovingly. "Just because you read so many mystery books and enjoy watching mysteries on TV doesn't mean that someone in Willow Bend is capable of such a devious thing."

"Well, it was just a thought . . . "

"You're not Miss Marple, my dear Gracie. Nor do we have here Cabot Cove's requisite murder per week—not even an occasionally attempted one. Maybe before you start hunting for clues, you'd better first consider reading other things."

This was too much! Indignantly, she defended her taste in literature. "Look, Rick, a good mystery is refreshing; in what other genre can you routinely find right triumphing over wrong in today's world?"

She knew she shouldn't rise to the bait but, really, how could she keep from it? "No matter how rotten people can be, no matter what moral or ethical or spiritual rules are broken and seem to be gotten away with, by the end of most mystery novels the doers of evil get their comeuppance— they do get their just desserts."

All around her were fond grins, which she tried to ignore, but in a few more minutes they were all again deeply involved with the meeting, everyone apparently determined to stick to the agenda since they were running so late. Things from this point on went smoothly, and nearly all of the business was concluded when Paul phoned.

"Amy seems about the same to us, but the doctor and nurses seem certain she's *stabilized*."

Gracie, who'd taken the call, heard this news with gratitude. "Good! Maybe it was our prayers. Anyway, the meeting's nearly finished, so I'm planning to come back there. Is there anything I can bring—or do?"

"Thanks, Gracie, but I can't think of a thing we need. And, since I've decided to stay here with Roy and Linda for the rest of the night, there's no need for you to come."

"I'd be glad to, Paul—to relieve *you*, if for no other reason."

"Thanks for that, too, but you go home and get your rest. You may be needed even more in the morning."

"Oh?" She wasn't sure she liked the sound of that. "Why did you say that?"

"I'm—not sure, but the doctor's just been in again, this time asking questions about the possibility of Amy having been 'given something,' and that has her parents really upset. I'm hoping it turns out to be just some kind of a 'bug,' some virus or something, but at the moment, not knowing for certain just what they're dealing with, everyone's concerned."

"Yes," she said softly. "I'm sure they would be."

She didn't mention what their pastor had just told her, however, to the board members.

Gracie had been too tired to bother taking all of her leftovers home, but she did carry out the containers of soup. Now, returning to the peace of her own house, carried them into her kitchen. There wasn't enough refrigerator space for both, so she transferred the contents into smaller dishes. She'd divide them into portions-for-two packets tomorrow, and place them in the freezer.

Uncle Miltie was already in his room with the light out, so she tried to be quiet. Gooseberry, on the other hand, must have had enough sleep, and kept trying to lead her to the door for a walk or to his bowl to beg for a treat. "Sorry, Gooseberry, but I've had a big day and am not as spry as you right now," she told him, keeping her voice low. "Try me again in the morning, when we'll both be ready for a jaunt."

# Three

AND SHE WAS. It was another gloriously beautiful day, cool and crisp, but not cold—a perfect day for a four-mile power walk, with Gooseberry accompanying her. She often thought that her seven-year-old cat acted more like a puppy in some ways, going at least twice as far as his mistress by circling her, walking between her feet, and checking out cans sitting along the street awaiting the arrival of the garbage man.

He was fascinated by everything, scraps of paper, a styrofoam cup, a small sock—and, today, something in the shrubbery. He soon caught up with Gracie and laid a no-longer struggling, very dead gray mouse in front of her. With the toe of her shoe, she nudged it over to the inner edge of the sidewalk—then deliberately paid attention to other things as Gooseberry disposed of it.

One important advantage of coming out so early was that only the serious walkers were about, matching her obvious briskness. This made it easier to just wave or call a greeting to them and to those leaving for work, instead of having to chat.

Another benefit was that she was able to do some of her best thinking at this time—this morning's, not surprisingly, largely concerning the young choir member for whom she'd been praying.

To the best of her knowledge, everyone liked Amy—or at least, didn't *dis*like her. She was quiet, good-humored, and never pushy—or at least that's how she seemed to Gracie. She had to recognize, however, that a girl *could* be different at school or other places.

Amy recently had been helping in the Sunday school nursery, or so Gracie believed. She hadn't been checking on her, so she couldn't be positive. Could there be a clue there?

Amy's mother was the high school librarian, and had been ever since they came here, which must have been at least five or six years by now. Her dad was a manager with Ace Electronics, a high-tech company on the edge of town. Gracie had hardly spoken to Mr. Cantrell until last night—and felt she still didn't know much about him.

According to Pastor Paul, what had seemed to disturb him most was the physician's questions about the possibility of someone wishing her harm. *If* there had been intentional injury done to Amy, which still seemed most unlikely, when might it have taken place? At school? It couldn't have been accomplished at home or at church—could it?

But *supposing* it had been at church, who there might possibly have a motive? The only person who could conceivably have one would be Estelle—and Gracie was not about to even think of that! It was too ludicrous to imagine, even if she obviously longed to sing Amy's solo.

Estelle, after all, was a good woman. They'd known one another for years and Gracie couldn't think of any really "wrong" thing she'd ever done. (Of course, to any reader of mystery novels, that alone could qualify her as the prime suspect—but for the moment Gracie wasn't going to give that idea any room in her mind!)

Or, still considering what she kept reassuring herself was impossible—that the choir rehearsal was the scene of the crime—might whatever happened have been meant for someone else, with Amy *not* the intended victim!

It wasn't so easy following in the footsteps of Jessica Fletcher! Here she was, thinking of others who might have done something, but what were they thinking, in the meantime, about *her*? Remember, she told herself, it was you who prepared the soups in your own kitchen. And in the church she had not only fixed the beverages, but also laid out all the ingredients for sandwiches. Might she be considered as much a suspect as anyone else? Perhaps *more* so?

Or, what was much more bearable, perhaps there had been no foul play at all? Wasn't it possible that Amy simply had fallen victim to some peculiar, not to mention *rare* virus, like those that keep manifesting themselves suddenly and making headlines? One of these had been reported in their own paper not that long ago, so that's probably what it was.

It was a relief to come up with that thought—but only insofar as Amy was concerned. That would be the good news. The *bad* news was that, should that prove to be the case, there'd almost certainly be a number of others coming down with it, too.

Wouldn't it be incredible if this case should end up in the province of some national clearinghouse, like the CDC, the Center for Disease Control, which collects and disseminates such information so word can get out to physicians and hospitals?

She walked quickly back to her own street and saw a car parked in front of her house. As she got closer, she realized it was the pastor's, causing her to hurry even more, eager for news. Paul was in the kitchen with her uncle, who was just plunking down the big crockery cookie jar on the table after having gotten each of them a can of cola from the refrigerator.

"And we were so thirsty that our throats were like sandpaper. . . ." Uncle Miltie was sharing one of his World War II stories—which still surprised her. Until the last five or ten years he'd refused to talk about these memories, and still wouldn't get drawn into any discussion or description of his long stay in a prison camp.

This time he was going on about his experiences during the Battle of the Bulge, and Paul was listening respectfully.

But Gracie knew how tired their pastor must be, after staying at the hospital all night, and soon managed to interrupt. "Can I distract you long enough to offer French toast or omelets?" Paul declined, saying he'd be leaving in just a few minutes; he'd got no sleep, and was looking forward to dropping off for several hours before a scheduled interfaith luncheon.

He'd simply wanted to reassure Gracie with the report that Amy appeared to be somewhat better, though still not herself. "She seems confused," he reported. "To me, she even seems scared of something, but of *what* I just don't know."

As Gracie walked with him to his car, she tried out on him some of her recent thoughts, and he didn't make fun of her or tease her about amateur detecting. He even nodded and said he'd come up with similar explanations, himself. However, he didn't share any additional theories, which made her feel guilty, as though she'd been gossiping or something.

At least she hadn't mentioned the only person she'd thought of who might conceivably harbor a motive. Estelle truly could be difficult, and her feelings easily hurt, yet she could be almost saccharine-sweet at other times, especially when dealing with the younger singers. Like Amy.

Gracie tried to push this thought out of her mind, to erase any suspicion as to Estelle's jealousy trying to do away with solo or duet competition. She even felt her conscience pricked for not giving Estelle even one of those spots for Sunday.

But how could she? Every single person in the choir had

been so generous with time and effort that it would hardly be fair to allow Estelle, with all her airs, extra opportunity to mess things up.

She hoped, of course, that the woman wouldn't drop out of the choir again, as she had two or three years ago when showing her displeasure at "being passed over again." It had taken a lot of effort then, especially on the part of Gracie and the thirty-five-year-old Turner twins, Tish and Tyne, to smooth her ruffled feathers.

Barb, in order to keep peace, had deliberately allowed her a few solo parts since then, and in July and August, when the choir as a whole was "off," Estelle had been asked to sing a solo each month. That opportunity would have been more rewarding had she not tried so hard to show off what she felt certain was her superior talent and ability. As it was, the smiles on the congregants' faces or behind their hands and bulletins seemed to sometimes be more of humor than appreciation.

Gracie drove Uncle Miltie to Barry's Barber Shop for a trim of his still-thick gray hair, and while he waited for his turn, she crossed the street to see what might still be warm from Abe Wasserman's ovens. She'd been hoping for a special coffee cake—but the cheesecake looked pretty tempting, as well.

As usual, she sat up at the counter while talking with Abe about many things: books they'd read recently, the price of cheese and other ingredients, the beauties of the season—

and, of course, the emergency situation involving Amy Cantrell.

Abe had just removed crisply thin honey cookies from the oven and, walking around to sit, perched one stool away, so the plate of still-hot treats was within easy reach for both of them.

She'd remembered that Amy had occasionally worked part-time for Abe. "She's been a big help to me these past two summers, and sometimes on Saturdays, and I've come to care a lot for her," he said. "Like a sort of granddaughter to me," he told her, "sweet and lovely with a rosebud air— and just as easily crushed."

She waited for him to continue and, focusing past her left shoulder, toward the front door, he finally did. "I did notice in her something continually a little tense, a kind of low level anxiety. I couldn't figure out the reason, though it was always there. And she has this—this *need* to be liked, to be loved—yet at the same time seems afraid to open herself to people."

He then looked directly into her eyes. "Why is this, Gracie? Do you have an explanation? Am I crazy?"

"Now that I think of it, I suppose I noticed it, too, but tried to tell myself I was imagining things. So I didn't pursue the matter, though perhaps I should have."

He nodded in agreement. "Why not now? Before it's too late."

Amy was only seventeen. Could someone be merely trying

to scare her? To kill her? Or, could the problem stem from something within herself? Were Gracie and Abe worrying about nothing? Maybe, going back to the virus theory, there *was* no "problem" as such, and they were headed off the deep end, just two overprotective snoops.

Suddenly remembering that Uncle Miltie might be waiting for her across the street, Gracie smiled in amusement at the thought, and told Abe she had to go. He asked her to wait a few seconds and, going back around the counter, he took a paper from beneath the cash drawer, but held onto it saying, "You know, Gracie, Amy was always punctual. But during the last week of summer, just before school started, she was barely making it on time. And she seemed to be more nervous, more uptight or edgy than before.

"I tried talking to her—but got nowhere. Then I figured it might have something to do with her boyfriend, which would be none of my business, except that it *was* my business she was being late for."

"Oh? I never saw her with a boyfriend, certainly not at the Youth Fellowship or its group activities."

He nodded to show he'd heard, even if he had not responded directly. "Well, it wasn't actually a boy. I got a few glimpses of him, and he's dark-complexioned and of medium height and weight—and obviously older. He'd sometimes drop her off here, and also pick her up after work. He'd never come in, though, and when I told her I'd like to meet her friend, she got real flustered—and asked me not to say anything to anyone about him."

Gracie frowned. "I don't like the sound of that!"

"Me, neither. That's why, when she was ready to leave that Saturday, I sneaked out the side door to check him out—but all I could see was the fairly new, gray Ford. And *this*," laying the paper on the counter in front of her, "is the number on the license plate—a Florida license."

She reached across to remove the pen from his breast pocket, and copied the series of digits onto the corner of her napkin. Tearing it off, she then carefully placed the paper in her wallet and after asking a few more questions, said she must pick up Uncle Miltie.

However, suspecting that he was making the most of this time to try out some of his newer, but still awful jokes on his friends, Gracie hurried down a side street, intent on making another very important stop—at the police station—before getting him.

❧ 2

When she got back to the barbershop, her uncle was busy with one of his jokes: "A man asked his pastor if it was a sin to play golf on Sunday. The minister replied, 'Sir, the way you play golf, it's a sin every day!'" No one laughed more than her uncle.

She never actually told him that she'd gone nowhere but Abe's and didn't feel guilty when he presumed that. Anyway, the fact that she'd brought with her a dozen freshly baked honey-almond cookies helped take his attention from the time he'd waited.

She parked in her driveway and they went inside—and were almost relieved to find no messages had been left on the answering machine. Gracie considered calling the hospital but, not being a relative, feared she wouldn't be given any meaningful information about Amy's condition.

She also momentarily thought of calling Phyllis Nickolson, who was probably on the switchboard, for she seemed to know just about everything that went on at Keefer Memorial. She didn't, however, deciding instead just to drive on over to the hospital. It was likely she wouldn't be allowed in to see her young friend, but it might be harder for them to refuse her request if she just showed up there.

Everything would depend on which nurses were on duty.

She went back to where she'd parked Fannie Mae, wondering if she had subconsciously planned to go see Amy when pulling into the garage as she almost always did. She just loved this dark blue, shiny oversized vehicle that Elmo had bought for her right after some dear friends were killed in their small economy car.

"They didn't stand a chance against that pickup truck the drunk was driving," he'd insisted. "You're the most important person in my life, Gracie, and I want to keep you forever. . . ."

She'd had no idea that *her* "forever" of keeping him with

her would be just five more years. And his death had happened in an accident, not with another person's vehicle, but
on a deserted stretch of road only five miles from here.

To the best of her knowledge, he had never before fallen
asleep when driving. Yet, coming back to her from Chicago at
almost two in the morning, with an almost-full moon and
that stretch of road in good shape, with nothing to obstruct
his view as he came around that curve. . . .

Might it have made a difference had *he* been driving
Fannie Mae?

But she would not, could not let herself dwell on that.

She turned on the radio to the station featuring Golden
Oldies and started to harmonize along with those songs she
knew well, humming when she forgot some of the words. It
didn't really matter if the selections were from the fifties or
the sixties or seventies or even later.

Or earlier, for that matter: She liked almost all of them.

She was taking the long way to the hospital, along rural
roads she and Elmo had often wandered. There were times
like this when he still seemed so very near, so close that she
could almost touch him, or at least talk with him.

Both of them had been strong willed, so there were of
course some disagreements, even an occasional flare-up—but
there had not been a single day after they first had met that
she hadn't loved him.

They often went for drives, or for long walks together, and
they had such big plans for their future, for his retirement—

but all of these were based on the assumption that they would be doing things *together*, not having one of them left alone!

*How I wish we could talk things over, El! This situation with Amy has me so upset, so worried. You were the one who could look at things from a dozen different perspectives while I was hung up on just one or two. How I need your wisdom now, dear.*

*You didn't know Amy and, anyway, she'd have been only twelve when you were killed. Come to think of it, I guess I didn't know her then, either, but have had the chance now to see her grow and develop, and I do care about her. . . .*

She was almost there, going down the street on which the hospital stood. Gracie believed wholeheartedly in what she was doing, yet recognized that she was instinctively still looking for the right path to take. As she turned into the parking area, she sent up a silent heartfelt prayer for Amy— and also for herself, that she would say and do whatever was best for her young friend.

She couldn't, in fact, have asked for a better nurse to be on duty than Nancy Bixler, who had known Gracie all her life. "Amy doesn't seem to be in any pain, but just wants to lie there," Nancy told her. "Even sipping water or juice through a straw or from a glass is apparently just too much trouble, and she can't be persuaded to try to eat a bite. Not of *any*thing."

"Would you let me talk to her?" Gracie asked. "I don't know

if I can get through, but I'd sure welcome the opportunity. . . ."

There was only a moment's hesitation before the nurse opened the ICU door. "You might as well; you can't do worse than we have." But then, as they started inside, she added, "She did seem to perk up a little when her parents were with her for a few minutes. Perhaps seeing another familiar face will help."

Amy looked so young, pale, and vulnerable that Gracie ached for her. Turning to the nurse, she whispered that maybe they should just let her sleep—but at the mention of her name, Amy's blue eyes slowly opened and looked right at Gracie.

Gracie reached out and took her hand—she couldn't help herself. She sat on the thin blanket next to her and stroked her arm gently. She was sure she felt a momentary responsive squeeze before Amy's eyelids closed again. Gracie told herself it might have been an unplanned or unintended sequence, but suspecting it to have been a deliberate decision not to communicate, she sent up another quick, inaudible prayer for help.

She told Amy how sorry she was about what had happened, then talked about her parents and her pastor staying with her throughout the night.

None of this got any response so, remembering Amy's love of animals, she related some of the silly things Gooseberry had done recently, and how Gracie sometimes thought there must be a dog's soul inside of him. "After all, he follows me everywhere, and he loves dog biscuits—and tussles playfully with Charlotte, Marge's shih-tzu!"

That finally earned the shadow of a smile from the silent patient, just a small flicker of response, but enough to encourage Gracie to think of other Gooseberry-inspired anecdotes. She even admitted her own squeamishness at witnessing the ultimate end of that gray mouse this morning, confessing that she'd had to turn away!

Having allowed Gracie to chatter on, Amy finally made a comment of her own, and her hand again seemed to squeeze back. "I like Gooseberry's coming right up to me. He rubs against my legs and lets me pet him."

Just at that moment Nancy came back in and tilted the top of the bed upward, something Gracie gathered had previously been protested. She understood that any cooperation they could get on Amy's part indicated improvement.

Gracie assumed that Nancy's arriving at that time was a reminder of her own promise to stay for only five minutes. Upon leaving, she still knew nothing more about what brought on the "attack" last night. She'd not even dared to bring that up directly, for leading questions, no matter how carefully worded, were difficult to frame so they didn't sound prying, had been ignored.

But at least she was now more confident about Amy's recovery. Their prayers seemed in the process of being answered, for Gracie sensed that Amy, deep with herself, was struggling to return to her previous state of mental and physical health.

🙾

Gracie closed the garage doors, and, as she walked back toward her house more slowly than usual, realized that Uncle Miltie had been out doing more pruning. She felt exhausted, and had even considered not stopping at the church to pick up the leftovers that had been left in the refrigerator there last night.

She normally enjoyed meal planning and preparation, whether it was a simple snack for herself, a dinner for Uncle Miltie and herself, a Sunday supper for friends, or a Thanksgiving banquet. But right now it was good to just re-heat some of the vegetable soup and make them each a sandwich

Uncle Miltie had jotted down a phone number for her to call, but couldn't say who it was. "He didn't give his name, Gracie, but it sounded sort of like Herb Bower. He said he needed you to call as soon as you got back."

*Needed?* She didn't want to ask if that was the exact word used, but punched in the numbers right away. A woman's voice answered after the very first ring, then Herb Bower, Willow Bend's chief of police, was on, asking, "Have you mentioned to anyone that number you brought me?"

"No, I haven't." She resisted asking why. "Have you been able to make some identification?"

He didn't answer that. "Look, Gracie, I'd appreciate this

remaining just between you and me at this point, okay?"

"Of course, but...."

"And the same goes for Abe's mentioning and describing the man interested in Amy. But please, if there's anything else you think of—if you get *any* more information, even the smallest, seemingly inconsequential things, I'd appreciate your passing it on."

"I don't know what that could be, but yes, I'll do that." She started to ask another question, but it went unanswered or, rather, since she'd heard that tiny click, she realized he was no longer on the line.

For a moment she stood there looking down at the phone. She knew Herb better socially than professionally, but felt sure he'd not deliberately go around trying to antagonize or upset people by hanging up on them. Perhaps he'd been interrupted by someone coming into the office, or maybe he had so much on his mind that he didn't even recognize that this could be interpreted as rudeness.

Could his abruptness have anything to do with Amy's case? Could things be getting even more complicated, rather than simpler? Had he learned anything about the identity of Amy's mysterious so-called friend? Could drugs possibly be involved? Murder? Espionage?

*Or have my years of devoted reading and watching mysteries done something to my senses—caused them to sort of kick in suddenly, making me suspicious of everything and everyone?*

She snorted in annoyance at even having those thoughts, and also at the unknown factors that were making her think them. None of it made any sense at all in friendly, peaceable Willow Bend!

*Tomorrow*, she promised herself, *I'm going back to the hospital and I'm simply going to find out from Amy who and what this friend is!"*

# Four

B UT A DIFFERENT NURSE, one she didn't know, was on duty when she turned up the next day, and stated authoritatively that only the immediate family could see Amy while she was still in intensive care. And that was *another* something to mull over. For Gracie had telephoned the Cantrells shortly after getting around that morning, and they'd been convinced Amy was much improved.

She returned home and got a load of laundry running while she swept, dusted, and worked at clearing away some of the other tasks that had been set aside in all the excitement, though not the sort of excitement one welcomes, she thought.

Finally, by early afternoon, she and Gooseberry were ready to start out on their walk, but with her mind on so many other things, Gracie wasn't paying much attention to where she was going until she noticed she'd headed off to one of the older parts of town. Begun some 150 years earlier as an area of residences for tradespeople and other upper-middle-class citizens, it was a longer route she seldom took.

Though the section had deteriorated in earlier years, during the last two or three decades most of the weathered old wooden houses had been given new windows and plantings and were re-sheathed with aluminum or vinyl siding, making it now one of the prettier neighborhoods of Willow Bend.

She always enjoyed having Gooseberry with her, even though some people looked frankly amused at seeing the big, Halloween-orange cat not only accompanying, but trotting right along with—and around—a red-haired, sixty-plus woman who was out there exercising so briskly!

She made a point of smiling at each of them; the problem for most of these folks was that they didn't have a cat like hers—as though anybody *could*!

Ah, yes, there was Amy's house up ahead, that large corner one with the wraparound verandah across the front and partway back on either side. It was all-white, white-on-white, trim and all—as were also the houses on either side of it.

Gracie slowed a little as she went by Fifth Street, then turned on Maple. There was the short driveway leading to their three-car garage; all of its doors were closed—as tightly shut as her mind seemed to be when it came to unraveling the situation with Amy!

She recalled having dropped off the girl off a number of times before she was old enough to drive—and even a few months ago brought her home after choir, when the car she sometimes drove was being repaired.

But she couldn't keep her mind on those past moments when she remained so obsessed with what had happened to Amy the other night. It had to have been just a bug, or some viral thing that hit her so suddenly—didn't it?

Yet she still had this odd feeling she was missing something—and she didn't like that one bit! *Is Amy in danger? Can there be some reason other than her physical condition, which could account for her still being in ICU when they say she's so much improved?*

She sucked in a deep breath of the morning shower-cooled air and deliberately stopped to look at a trellised rose at the edge of the Cantrell property, forcing herself to give it her full attention.

But this was no way to get the exercise she felt her body and mind needed! Straightening to her full height—she hoped she hadn't started getting shorter, as many people do as they age—she took several steps before realizing she was alone. At first she was almost amused, fully expecting Gooseberry to amble out of one of the plantings where he'd been checking for whatever he could find that might appeal to him.

She hoped it wouldn't be something alive or recently alive, like that mouse, which he'd obviously considered to be worthy of her praise. He'd been known to bring her chipmunks and moles or even (though more rarely, thank goodness) small snakes—which she'd informed him he need not do again, thank you!

Gracie retraced her steps for a short distance, but he didn't come bouncing out from behind the massed yellow coreopsis or the large bed of sturdy marigolds even when she called his name—something she recognized as an exercise in futility. Gooseberry did not feel obligated to come when she called—that being, she reminded herself, one good argument against her "theory" that, in spite of appearances, he was actually a dog!

She was annoyed. Time passed very quickly when she was striding along, but standing still or moving just a few steps made it almost stop. She should go on home without him—but knew she wouldn't, even though old-timers often told of cats finding their way home from miles away, even hundreds of miles.

And who was she to be thinking of others as old-timers? Even twenty or thirty years ago she thought people in their sixties were either already in or dangerously near being in that category. *Fortunately, I don't feel like anything that term indicates*, she thought. *And I don't believe I look or act like it either!*

She felt a rueful, self-disparaging expression creep across her face. Probably every reasonably healthy, fairly active person her age thought of herself or himself as being an exception to the description "elderly."

And that word set her mind off in another direction. She

must remember to tell Rocky that she didn't appreciate one of his newspaper staff—undoubtedly quite young—writing of an "elderly" man hurt in an accident last week, then finding as she read the article that the injured person was sixty-one! *Come on, Rocky! Don't let them make us "elderly" before our time!*

Although her thoughts had been wandering, she'd also been keeping a vigilant eye out for that missing member of her household. Suddenly she saw him meandering down the very middle of the Cantrells' front sidewalk! There was something light-colored in his mouth, but it was only when he came closer that she realized it was a shell, a rather large one, actually, but not of a clam or oyster or mussel or whelk, which made up her entire familiarity with shells.

She reached down to take it from him, but he backed away, then deliberately kept beyond arm's reach as he preceded or walked behind or beside her on the way home.

Gracie was annoyed with him—and with herself for letting him get away with acting like this. It felt like condoning an act of thievery, except that her cat couldn't understand that concept—and she could only guess from whose property it might have come.

She'd assumed when first seeing him that he'd emerged from the plantings in front of Amy's porch. However, he'd been gone long enough that he could have been at any of the neighbors', then come back that way.

"Where have you been, you curious cat?" she demanded. "Where did you get that? Is it one that somebody brought back from a visit to the seashore?" She hoped that wasn't the case, for that would mean it was treasured as a memento. *I'm going to hope someone bought fresh seafood, then threw out the shells.* "But, of course, you know the adage about what kills cats."

That it had been part of meal preparation surely was the answer, wasn't it? If so, it wouldn't hurt for Gooseberry to carry his rather unusual trophy back home if he wished. It seemed strange for him to bother with something like this, yet he'd done the same with certain other inanimate objects like going off with Uncle Miltie's screwdriver when he'd been right in the middle of fixing the garage door last week. And Gracie had long ago discovered that she couldn't leave a dust cloth lying around and expect to find it where it had been left.

She couldn't tell for sure, but assumed there was nothing within the shell. She smelled nothing rotten from this distance—however, *should* it be there, she supposed that might partially account for the cat's so proudly bearing it home.

They'd been walking along Maple Street for well over a block when a smooth-running gray Ford passed them, going in the same direction. With almost disbelief she saw—and she took out the torn-off piece of napkin to make sure—that the license plate had the same numbers as those she'd copied at Abe's!

What were the odds that the one car she'd been thinking about would pass by her here?

Uncle Miltie was more intrigued by Gooseberry's find than she was. Having been quite a fisherman, he knew most of the freshwater mollusks that could be found in the lakes and streams of Ohio and Indiana—but this was new to him. He was curious enough to look it up in the seashell guide he had on his shelves, along with other volumes about nature.

Gooseberry had marched right in with it and willingly gave it to her uncle—earning for himself a, "What a good cat you are!" and extra petting, which he obviously enjoyed. He even sat there beside Uncle Miltie at the kitchen table, as though interested in the search being conducted.

"I can't find any pictures *exactly* representing this one, Gracie, but these periwinkles look something like it." He read aloud the accompanying information, which mentioned a caveat about some of them being poisonous. "I wonder where he found it."

"Me, too. All I know is that he wasn't carrying it as we approached the corner of Fifth and Maple, where Amy lives." And that reminded her again of the gray car, which had to have passed that house shortly after she did.

Feeling rather foolish even while doing it, she made a phone call as soon as Uncle Miltie went back into the other room to watch a science fiction movie on one of the cable networks. "Hello, Herb, this is Gracie, and I'm sure this isn't at all what you had in mind when you told me to call about anything which might be unusual or suspicious. . . ."

She waited for his assurance that whatever she thought

was worth calling about was, indeed, bound to be significant. "Well, I was out for my daily walk—I went this afternoon, since it was raining this morning." *Oh dear, he's so busy and I'm just rambling, giving unnecessary information.*

"My cat went with me, as he usually does. We were going past Amy's house when Gooseberry disappeared for a while, then came back carrying a strange whitish shell."

*Get to the point, Gracie,* she scolded herself. *That's not what you were calling about!* "And then as we were coming up Fifth Street, maybe a block or so from Amy's, I saw a gray Ford— actually, *the* gray Ford, the one with those license numbers I gave you."

There was silence for a moment before Herb's voice asked, "And . . . ?"

"Well, uh—I didn't know if it was of interest that the mystery man may have been driving past Amy's house to check on her, or to . . . I don't know . . . it's like I just said, it was probably silly to call about such a minor thing."

"We can't consider anything 'silly' or 'minor' as of now, Gracie, so I'm glad you called—I really am."

"Do you suppose it's possible he was the one she'd planned to meet for a movie after the rehearsal? If he's on the level, I suppose he could be worried about her, and was cruising around trying to see her. . . ." But it was that "if" that was unsettling.

"That does represent a possibility," he replied, his tone giving no indication as to whether he thought that plausible.

She did not go on with the reverse of her supposition: if he were *not* on the level. "Have you heard anything recently about Amy's condition?"

"She's supposedly doing very well."

*Supposedly.* Everything with qualifications! "Will she be getting out of the hospital soon?"

"I'm not sure just when—but then I'm not the doctor."

"Something seems strange, Herb. Don't they usually, nowadays, take people out of ICU as soon as possible? Is she sicker than we've been led to believe?"

There was a small chuckle. "Remember me, Gracie? I'm a policeman, not a physician. I'm not about to get drawn into the usually's or what should be's of medical care."

She laughed, too. "That brings us back to the old saw about a little knowledge being a dangerous thing, right?"

"Right!"

But that wasn't the end of their conversation. He wanted to know, "Did you get the impression that the man might have noticed you?"

"From the time I saw his car, he kept looking straight ahead, not paying any attention to me nor turning toward me. But he probably did *see* me. How could he keep from seeing this red-haired woman and her pumpkin-colored cat striding along?"

Although Herb was good at asking questions and expecting a response, it was evident that it didn't work that way with her queries. Thus, she wasn't expecting it when a police car stopped in front of her house within the next half-hour and Herb appeared at her door to ask more about the shell, and to see it.

"It's probably not significant, Gracie," he told her—but despite saying that, he asked to take it with him. Uncle Miltie was the one who emphatically informed him that they wanted it returned. After all, he was still trying to find out what it was!

Gracie made an effort to relax, but received a number of calls through the evening—from nearly every one of the choir members, in fact. There seemed to be more and more nervousness, and mounting uncertainty, about tomorrow afternoon, especially, but about the morning service as well.

"Everything's going to be fine," she assured Tyne Anderson, one of the altos.

But Tyne wasn't easily convinced. "I just got off the phone with my sister, and we can't remember everything that was changed on those two numbers, like when we come in."

It wasn't surprising that this was a problem for Tyne, who never seemed able to count out the rhythm, the beats. "I remember seeing you penciling in the changes on your music, so I'm sure you'll do fine once you have that in front of you. And I'll be right there, like at rehearsal, helping you know when to begin."

"I—just don't know...."

"Please don't stew about it. We're all going to be at church early tomorrow, remember? That way we'll go over *Help Me to See Thee, Lord*, and we'll also be using it as our choir anthem in the morning.

"If people get there as soon as requested, I'm hoping we can run through that twice. And remember that we're staying long enough after Sunday school to sing through *Hallalujah, Save Us, Lord*—so we'll be able to work on anything that might still need a little polishing."

Tyne and Tish were now thirty-five years old but still known throughout the church and community as "The Turner Twins," probably because they were both blond and blue-eyed, were usually seen together, always wore girlish dresses and shoes, and liked the same things. They'd been married for perhaps seventeen years—Tyne to Bill Anderson, and Tish to John Ball—and were both giggly and unsure of themselves.

Gracie had tried several times to have Tish move into the soprano section. Although she might need some help in developing the top of her range, that section more often than not carried the melody—a big help for someone who couldn't get the hang of reading music!

However, Tish would not change seats, choosing to remain with her sister, also an alto.

When Gracie picked up the phone the next time, however, the caller's attitude offered a welcome change of pace. "Hi, Gracie, it's Rick. How are things going for you this lovely evening?"

"Hel-*lo*, Rick. It's great to hear your cheerful voice—a wonderful contrast from those in the choir who are so worried or pessimistic about tomorrow."

He laughed. "Did you tell them that faint hearts ne'er win awards?"

She was so relieved by his attitude that she sank onto a kitchen chair. "I would have had I thought of it. Okay if I steal it?"

"That's impossible, Gracie! It's given to you. Be my guest."

"I'm glad you called, Rick, I wanted to tell you how much I appreciate and thank you for taking on the special music. It was sorta thrust upon you, but we had to do something about those sections."

"No problem at all. You know I love to sing." Rick Harding had been sent to Indiana by his computer company when they were opening their new division here. There weren't a lot of other African Americans in Willow Bend, but the new dentist practicing with Dr. Comfort had come with his wife, a nurse/anesthetist, and there were two teachers and at least a dozen students now in the school system.

Gracie couldn't speak for the whole community, but there didn't appear to be any prejudice, and everyone here in this church had come to love Rick, his wife and their two-year-old daughter. Of all the voices, his was the most exceptional, and he could not only read music but had previous experience in choirs much larger and more prestigious than theirs.

Unlike Estelle, however, he never tried to throw his weight

around. Even now, he didn't appear worried or troubled. He just asked, "Is there anything I can do to help you tomorrow, Gracie? I know you have things under control, but I'm available if there's anything that needs done."

She sighed, this time from thankfulness, not tension. "I didn't realize how much the downheartedness of some others was beginning to get to me. Thanks for the pick-me-up."

"Anytime." He chuckled. "This is great. I'm not used to receiving two thank-you's in one day."

"Well, let's really make your day, then. I want especially to thank you for not only knowing what to do with Amy last night, but doing it. She might not have made it if we'd had to wait for the ambulance."

She thought his momentary hesitation was going to lead to his saying he hadn't done anything that special but, instead, there was a question. "I wasn't sure what was happening—I *still* don't know, do you?"

She shook her head, even though he couldn't see that. "I know they've been doing a number of tests, but if they have significant results, I've not been informed."

They talked about several other things before Gracie asked, "Do you do much research on the Web?"

"Sure—quite a bit."

"Well, I'm practically computer illiterate, so could I ask a favor?"

"Of course. What is it, more recipes?"

She laughed, remembering that at one of their rehearsals a

year ago somebody had mentioned a craving for her grand-mother's "light dumplings." When none of the women had been able to come up with a recipe for them, it was Rick who had solved the problem by going on-line. The whole choir thanked him when, the following week, Gracie surprised everyone with this unexpected old-fashioned dish.

"No, not a recipe this time—it's for a shell Uncle Miltie thinks might be a winkle, he says, or a periwinkle. My cat, Gooseberry, is always finding things and bringing them to me—but it's my uncle who's intrigued by this particular one, which he can't find in his field guides."

"Bring it with you to church in the morning, so I'll know what I'm looking for when making the search. I'm sure we can come up with something."

That sounded so simple—but she'd never tried to do it herself. "If you succeed, your reward will be more light dumplings, okay?"

"It's a deal!"

"But don't worry if you can't find it—I'll make them again soon because I'm getting hungry for them, too."

It was after hanging up that she remembered lending the shell to Herb.

Later, after supper, Gracie began going over her notes for her Sunday school class the next morning, but errant thoughts kept creeping into her mind. She tried disciplining them, but when they continued to intrude she got up and headed for the living room. "How about some ice cream?"

Uncle Miltie looked over the top of his glasses. "What flavors are there?"

"We always have vanilla, but there's also Cookies 'n' Cream, and Butter Pecan. Take your pick."

It was no surprise when he chose the Cookies 'n' Cream—he usually did when it was in the lineup. Since he was in the middle of watching a nature program, she joined him in the living room for the end of the segment on seals. Although not one for watching football, golf, game shows, or science fiction, all of which he was partial to, she did sometimes join him for history, travel, or nature ones.

She and Elmo had had much more similar interests.

She went back to the kitchen when the phone rang again. This time it was Marge, somewhat gloomy because, "There's not a thing to do here in Willow Bend on a Saturday night—not when you're unattached!"

"Oh, I don't know." Gracie knew if she let Marge start, she'd cry on her shoulder for a good chunk of what was left of the evening. "Uncle Miltie and I are sitting here in front of the TV finishing off bowls of ice cream. What more could anyone want?"

"Oh, Gracie! You, too, must get lonely!"

"If you mean missing Elmo, of course I do, and always will. But I don't wallow in it, dear friend. There are too many things in life—good things, I'll have you know—for me to lose out on if I allow myself to stay in the dumps!"

What finally happened was that Marge came over for "one game of Scrabble"—which became "just one more" when Uncle Miltie joined them at the kitchen table. This was his favorite game—and he almost won this time, too, but had a "Q" left to be played—and no available "U" anywhere.

Marge's win got her out of the doldrums, and she only partly in jest said they were poor sports when Gracie, yawning openly, started to put things back in the box. "I'm bushed, Marge," she explained, "and I'm heading for bed within the next ten minutes."

Marge pretended offense. "I thought we were friends, and here you are, practically pushing me out your door!"

"And if you leave peaceably and soon, the 'practically' will remain in that sentence," Gracie responded, putting their cups, bowls, and spoons in the dishwasher.

Marge shook her head ruefully as she started for the door. "Well, so much for friendship. I finally win one game and get thrown out of the house."

They could hear her still laughing as she stepped off the porch and started across the yards. "You're an excellent niece, Gracie," Uncle Miltie said as his arm circled her shoulders. "And you're one terrific friend to many people."

She felt humbled at his saying that. "I have such wonderful people as friends, Uncle Miltie. And as relatives."

He nodded. "It takes one to recognize others, my dear."

# Five

S HE'D EXPECTED TO READ a few chapters of a new mystery before going to sleep, but made it through only part of the first one. It was with amazement that she opened her eyes to daylight. Those numbers on the digital clock couldn't be right, could they? 7:42?

She looked at her watch, and got up immediately. She was expected to be at church in forty-eight minutes and she still had to shower and dress! Thank goodness her hair was naturally curly and that she still had enough natural color so her skin required only the lightest cosmetic emphases.

Tish and Lester were pulling into the parking area at the same time she got there, and Don arrived right after them. Gracie looked around as she entered the church, seeing excitement in everyone's eyes and hearing it in their voices. Somehow, thankfully, the negativity with which the last rehearsal had been conducted seemed dispelled. Instead, an enthusiastic we-can-do-it attitude permeated the place.

Paul didn't sing with them; as he'd put it when asked to join them, he had enough to do as pastor on a Sunday morning. But he was in and out of the back room as Barb played and the choir went through the anthem for the morning.

Gracie beamed at them. "You're wonderful! Positively marvelous!" she cried, bringing her palms together in applause. "There's nothing that I saw or heard that needs further work, but—well, I didn't tell you I was doing it, but I recorded this run-through on tape."

She glanced at her watch to make sure they had time for what she was about to suggest. "I'm going to play it back to you now. Pay special attention to your own parts, but also to others. *If* we need to go over one or two specific sections before we sing it straight through one more time, we will do so."

Don Delano did ask Barb to play one short passage, in order to make sure he was getting his baritone part just right, and then Rick requested help with the four-part harmony— which Gracie was quite sure was a request being made more for the altos than himself.

"In the beauty of Your world and in a baby's smile,
Whether I am far away or at home for a while,
Whether I am rich or poor, with pennies or a hoard,
Whatever my condition, help me to see Thee, Lord. . . ."

It was the final, FINAL rehearsal of *Help Me to See Thee, Lord*—and not one person missed a note and nobody came in at the wrong time. "We are READY!" Gracie cried, clasping her hands above her head in a victor's stance.

And the others responded, "We are READY!"

*Yes, God, I do see that only You could have changed the outlook, the mood of all these people overnight! Thanks . . . !*

Gracie hoped and prayed this enthusiasm would hold through the Sunday school period, which was to begin in a few minutes with her class meeting here in this room. Somebody had taken care of making the coffee and heating water for tea, so a number of people had already filled their mugs and were seated in a large circle.

Amy's father had come with his wife today, a first for Sunday school, although he was almost always there for church. Gracie asked Linda and Roy Cantrell to fill them in on their daughter's condition, and everyone was pleased to hear that Amy was apparently much better.

No one else seemed puzzled at her still being in intensive care, and Gracie didn't feel she should raise that question. They were all concerned, though, so Gracie led a brief prayer before getting into the lesson.

Jim Thompson was in her class today, too, along with the Cantrells and nineteen others. He was often on police duty on Sunday mornings, or else admitted to being in bed at that time, following an extra-long Saturday shift.

Gracie briefly brought up to speed those who had not been there for the study of the very beginning of the Christian church, the book of Acts—one of her favorites.

She'd read it many times, and now shared with the class the way each reading could offer new understanding and insights. Today's lesson was a continuation of last Sunday's, when Stephen, one of the seven deacons chosen by other followers of Christ, was giving his defense in the Temple.

Gracie filled in some of the background before getting a discussion going about how to know what *is* right—especially when everyone else thinks you're wrong. What must it have been like for Stephen's parents, his friends, and those who loved him?

Today's portion dealt with his being stoned to death—not for something he had done wrong, but because he'd tried to do what was *right*.

Several in the class were outspoken, but she was concerned about others who withdrew, looking down at their hands, or at a corner of the room, or out a window. Amy's mother reached out to touch her husband's sleeve, but he drew away, not acknowledging her gesture, nor looking at her, just holding in both hands the quarterly, thirteen printed lessons for adults, covering a three-month period. Gracie didn't have time to think about it right then, though suspected she would later.

The class was drawing to its close, a time always accompanied by prayer, so Gracie included a number of known needs—including Amy. ". . . And we know that nothing like this affects only the patient, Lord, any more than Stephen's murder concerned only him. So please be with her mother and father, and surround them and all the others we've prayed for, with Your love, Your protection, and Your peace. In Jesus' name, Amen."

Several members made a point of inviting the Cantrells to stay for the worship service, but they said they must go: ". . . We want to be with Amy."

"Give her my love, and assure her I'm continuing to pray for her," Gracie requested. "I'll be there to visit either today or tomorrow. . . ." But by then she had to hurry with preparations for the worship service, since Barb had already gone into the sanctuary and was playing the organ.

Gracie heard Estelle say, "Poor dear Amy, to be missing this day she worked so hard for!" and quickly felt guilty for being judgmental. Her very first reaction had been that the woman was exhibiting her sugar-wouldn't-melt-in-her mouth persona again—that she was trying to show everyone how generous and wonderful she was.

She wanted to banish this unkind thought, but it just would not fade away. She even had a mental picture of Estelle reaching her arm up in an alluring manner, adjusting the halo, which she so assiduously tried to keep polished.

However, following Paul's brief but meaningful prayer with the choir, it was easy for her and the others to let the smiles within their hearts show on their faces, as robed and *ready*, they lined up and processed into the stained-glass brightness.

Gracie wasn't quite as calm as she wished, and suspected some of the others were nervous, too. The service, however, was going smoothly, as usual, for Paul, who had come to serve here three years earlier, had a knack for organization, and everything fit together beautifully—the call to worship, the congregational singing, the scripture, everything.

It was time for the tithes and offerings to be received, and two of the older men and two teens slowly went back to the aisles. Then came the time for everyone to rise and sing the *Doxology* and for those who'd collected the offerings to return to their seats. And everyone else was seated, also.

Usually the choir members rose as one at this point, with no announcement, but today Paul mentioned that the number they were about to sing, *Help Me to See Thee, Lord*, was their anthem-of-choice, which would next be heard at the competition that afternoon at Waxmire Tabernacle. He hoped everyone would try to be there in support of these faithful people who used their talents and time to provide the excellent music these congregants got to hear each Sunday morning.

As Barb played the first note, Gracie, sitting in the front row, stood up, as did all of their choir members. They moved forward, positioning themselves so the back row was on the platform, the middle row on the wide steps, and the last ones in front of them, on the sanctuary's carpet. Just as rehearsed.

Gracie had moved over to stand front and center before

them. So now, looking forward, she gave an encouraging smile, moving both hands close in front of herself to give a double thumbs-up.

She nodded to Barb, and there was an immediate change in melody and tempo as the organist swung into the first bars of their anthem.

The singing started off perfectly, everyone in unison, the music and the words clear and easily understood. Most of it was in four-part harmony, but there were those several breaks when only one or two voices were featured. There was not a missed beat or muffled word.

And then there was the final, harmonious *Amen*.

There was a moment of silence, without so much as a rustling paper, and Gracie wondered if maybe they hadn't done as well as she'd thought. But then someone started clapping, then more and more as spontaneous applause rang out from their own congregation!

This did not happen very often in the Eternal Hope Community Church, and Gracie had a moment of wondering whether it was due to people responding to the message of their music or to their delivery—or possibly to the pastor's having mentioned that this was one of the two numbers they'd sing this afternoon.

Whatever the reason, every member of the choir was beaming as they returned to their seats.

*Thank You, Lord*, she breathed silently. *Even if we don't place in the competition, this has been a most wonderful, memorable experience today!* And she surreptitiously blotted a tear from each eye as Paul began his sermon.

Some members came up front after the service, telling individual members and the whole group how splendid the music had been, and that they were rooting for them. What was most thrilling to Gracie was how many promising, after hearing them this morning, that they were definitely going to be at Waxmire Tabernacle, on the other side of town, for the competition—despite not having considered that earlier.

No one thought it necessary again to go over the number they'd just sang so beautifully, but they wanted to run through the other a couple of times. It was, therefore, a little later than usual when Gracie and Uncle Miltie ate lunch. Afterwards, she called the hospital.

"Oh, that's great!" She was delighted to learn that Amy was no longer in intensive care. "What room has she been moved to?"

There was a slight pause before the person said, "Just a moment, please."

She heard the murmur of voices, then a briskly efficient voice was asking, "May I help you?"

"I understand that Amy Cantrell has been discharged from ICU, and I just wanted to know what room she's in."

"This is Mrs. Jackson. To whom am I speaking, please?"

*What difference does that make?* But she answered the question, "I'm Grace Parks, a friend of Amy's. I've visited her in

ICU, and just asked to what room she'd been moved." There seemed to be another pause, a longish one, which made her wonder why.

"I believe she is no longer a patient here at the hospital."

"What do you mean, she's no longer there? Has she gone home—been transferred to another hospital—what? How *is* she?"

"She seemed to be doing well."

Only one answer out of the three! "Then . . . ?"

"I'm sorry, Ms. Parks, but that is the only information I can give you. . . ."

There was a click on the line, indicating that Mrs. Jackson had hung up. Gracie felt light-headed. *I'm not catching the same virus or whatever Amy had, am I?* No, she was sure she wasn't. In fact, she recognized that she'd had this sensation before—when more upset than she was willing to acknowledge.

*What is going on?* The only thing she knew to do under this circumstance was to call the Cantrell home. She dialed—and became even more agitated at receiving no answer. There was not even an answering machine.

Well, they'd said they were going to see Amy right after Sunday school. Gracie would have thought that if they found that their daughter could leave the hospital, they'd have taken her home. On the other hand, considering how ill she'd been, and how little she'd eaten since being admitted, if Amy asked to stop for a snack on the way back to her house, they might have done so. Yet that scenario just didn't seem to fit with what she knew of this family.

On the other hand, *should* Amy be in trouble of any kind, Gracie could never forgive herself if she didn't at least try to help, even if she was pretty sure the Cantrells wouldn't welcome her intrusion.

She drove to their house, noting that the garage doors were shut again, and everything looked the same as the last time she saw it. She parked at the curb, got out, and walked up the sidewalk to the door, but no one came in response to her pressing on the doorbell a second and third time. She'd heard the ringing, so knew even as she then pounded on the door that such an effort was futile.

Still, she decided to walk all the way around the house. If the parents did any gardening, it was possible they might be out back.

They were not.

She even knocked on the side door of the garage but, as she expected, there was no answer.

*So what should I do now, Lord? I'm still trying to do what I think is right, but if there's something more, please show it to me.*

She went back to her car, and just sat there, thinking. *I don't want to make an ocean out of a mud puddle, as Uncle Miltie would say, and I don't have an awful lot of time because of the choir contest, but I'm here now, and available. Please, Lord, help me know what to do.*

Well, she supposed she should first of all call the police station. Thank goodness she had a good memory for numbers: She punched in the right one and Herb himself picked up on the first ring. She blurted out that she believed Amy to be missing, and how she'd failed when trying to reach the girl's parents, and. . . .

"Gracie—just a minute, Gracie."

"But. . . ."

"I know that she's left the hospital, and that you were making inquiries."

*How did you know I was asking questions?* "Is she okay? Do you know where she is?"

This time his response did not come as quickly, and even then it was not an answer: "Where are you right now?"

"In my car, in front of the Cantrell house, and. . . ."

"Could you drive over here to the station?"

"Well, sure, I can. But why?"

"Just come, as soon as you can."

"Okay, but. . . ."

"Park in the back, please—and tell no one where you're going, or why. . . ."

*Maybe I've been transported to Cabot Cove or St. Mary Mead after all!* And wouldn't Rick get a kick out of this particular scene? The director of their choir in the middle of what had all the earmarks of something cloak-and-daggerish—though it probably wasn't! "All right, Herb. I'll be there within two minutes."

And then, as she turned the ignition, she almost wished she'd not been quite that specific, timewise. Patsy, the little crippled girl who lived next door to the Cantrells, was coming out onto her porch, using her walker. She was waving at Gracie, and it looked as though she was beckoning her—but all Gracie had time for was to smile as she waved back.

She pulled away from the curb and kept going, watching Patsy recede in her rearview mirror. Although not understanding the rationale for such precautions as Herb had indicated, she came down the alley behind the station and parked there, where her car would probably not be seen.

Gracie was surprised to see the inconspicuous rear door of the building open as she got out of her car. She'd never had occasion to come back here before, but would hardly ever have noticed that, as there was no knob nor doorstep. And here was Herb, using the same motion she'd seen only a minute before, beckoning for her. "Come on in."

She glanced around as she walked toward him. "I feel like I'm in some suspense thriller or something."

"Or something?"

"I'm to come secretly, park here . . . and even come in through an unmarked door!"

"Well, yes." He reached for her arm. "But I'm not the ghoulish figure your fertile mind is probably conjuring up. Just a town policeman trying to do my job."

It was her turn to smile encouragement. "And there are many of us who sleep well at night for exactly that reason."

They turned left, into a medium-sized, neatly organized office she'd never seen before. But she wasn't looking at that right now, for Roy Cantrell was getting to his feet. "Thanks for coming, Mrs. Parks."

She looked from him to his wife, whose eyes and face looked as though she'd been crying. "You're welcome." *What more can I say when I haven't the faintest idea of why I've been asked to come?*

Herb indicated the third chair facing his desk, and went back to sit in his own as she took her seat. "Amy has disappeared, Gracie. We don't know how she got out of ICU with nobody seeing her, nor how she could have walked out of the hospital without raising suspicion and being stopped."

Gracie turned toward Linda. "She was still wearing one of those flimsy hospital gowns?"

"Not since yesterday." And the tears started again. "She'd been complaining about them, and got permission for us to bring her sweatpants and sweatshirts. Last night she was wearing the royal blue set, the one with colorful winter birds—cardinals and grosbeaks. I suppose she might be wearing the marigold-yellow one now . . . "

Herb was already punching in numbers on his phone, and asked the ICU nurse who answered, "What was Amy Cantrell wearing this morning? Yes, please *do* inquire—and also check on whether she left anything there, anything at all!"

Covering the mouthpiece with his hand, he muttered, "I can't believe I was that stupid—assuming she'd be dressed like a patient . . . !" But then he was listening to what the other person was telling him. After asking another question or two, he hung up.

"Okay, she was apparently wearing the blue outfit, since the yellow one's still there, along with her underclothing. There are personal toiletries, but no money—do you know if she had any?"

"Not much, a few dollars at most. She said she felt like a three-year-old if she didn't have at least some quarters. I tried to explain that the nurses would give her a soft drink or crackers or anything she wanted—but did end up giving her what change I had." She looked stricken. "If only I hadn't— but I never expected she'd do *this*!"

Gracie reached over and took her hand, then tried to warm it by holding it between her own, rubbing the back of it. "I suspect the nurses keep some record of ICU visitors, don't they? Do you know of any others besides the four of us, and our pastor?"

"They told me we were the only ones."

"She had to make contact with someone outside in order to sneak out of there—perhaps the man in the gray car?"

Herb started to shake his head as Roy demanded, "*What* man in a gray car?"

She let the officer explain what little they knew. Oddly, the part that seemed to bother Roy the most was that the car had a Florida license plate. "Have you checked out who it belongs to?"

"It's registered to an Andrew Hively and. . . ."

The man's face suddenly changed color. "He's—*here*?" The shock caused his voice to break.

"We're not positive of that. The car's make and model match the license plate, but we still don't have a good description of the man who's been driving it—and the car itself hasn't been seen since yesterday, although we've had an APB—an all points bulletin—out for it."

"Why didn't you tell me?" Roy demanded.

Herb was asking at the same time, "Why is his being here so important?"

This last query was the one answered. "He hates me! He's threatened me, hounded me and my family." Roy sank back into his seat, his voice little more than a moan, "Now he's back at it. Again."

Gracie asked, "Why does he hate you so much?" She realized as soon as the words came out that it should be the officer asking questions, but either way she wouldn't have been prepared for his reply.

"He accuses me of killing his father. He apparently believes that I did."

She was afraid she might have given an audible gasp, but nobody apparently noticed. Herb was asking, "And *did* you kill his father, Mr. Cantrell?"

"Of course not." He was so agitated that he was on his feet, but there was little room here in which to pace. "His dad, Tony—Anthony, that is—was my partner in a financial planning group, in Florida."

Linda was not even attempting to blot the tears running down her face. Herb started to reach for the box on the corner of his desk, but Gracie picked it up, pulled several tissues from it, and handed these to Linda as Roy continued.

"I trusted Tony implicitly—he was my best friend, and we did everything together. By the time I found out we were in trouble—when I first even suspected that things weren't as they should be, Tony was on a month's vacation, which was the first time he'd taken off for an extended period of time.

"I started noticing some—what I considered discrepancies, so tried to figure what was wrong. And then I brought in the best accountants in the state, hoping against hope that he— that Tony had not been stealing us blind!

"But he was! It turned out that even on that vacation, in Atlantic City and Las Vegas, he was using more of our money to try to win back his massive losses.

"He lost that, as well."

Gracie saw him pause behind his wife's chair, and her head leaned back against his chest as his hands came to rest on her shoulders, and her left hand, bare of any jewelry, rose to cover his.

"I had no choice but to go to the authorities and—by the time he got back it had become a certainty. At first he tried to bluff us, to use his carefully fictionalized records to confuse people.

"And when we began looking for it, we discovered a

paper trail so wide that at first it appeared to everyone that I had to have known about his embezzlement earlier.

"But I didn't! He was the one who took care of special accounts, and the elderly widows and singles adored him, and placed all their faith in him. They were the primary ones who were taken advantage of—multimillions of dollars siphoned off into supposedly safely secured accounts—with his name on them, so he could 'better take care of it for them.'"

Roy now looked physically ill. "He was of course not allowed near the accounts after that—though he tried desperately to get me to find some way of giving him access. He kept saying he could straighten out everything, that none of this was his fault.

"I felt almost as terrible about having to refuse him as in having been the one who started the investigation."

"So then he tried to pin it on Roy!" Linda was indignant. "Though *that* didn't work at all."

"Except with his family." Roy's voice had gotten lower and lower, until the last word was barely a whisper.

It was Linda who, in a pain-filled voice, added that, "If only Tony had toughed it out! Yes, there would certainly have been jail time, but . . . he'd always been the Golden Boy, the one on whom the sun would always shine.

"But when that light of adulation was shut off, his life, as he saw it, was over. He wrote a letter to his family, insisting he was innocent—and shot himself."

Gracie sat there stunned, staring at this woman and her husband. Herb looked down at the pen in his hand, then laid it down precisely, lined up perfectly with the edge of his pad. He looked straight at Linda, then Roy. "What happened then?"

He cleared his throat. "We saw it through as best we could, salvaging as much as possible for those who'd suffered such severe financial losses."

Linda nodded. "Most of what Tony stole proved to be unrecoverable but, again using his own records and investigating further, the authorities were able to prove where some of the stolen money went, in addition to what he used for gambling.

"But Andrew just never believed his father could have done what he was being accused of," Roy said. "Somehow he convinced himself it was all my fault—that I'd called in the accountants after I'd doctored the records to make Tony the fall guy for my thievery."

"Once he began denouncing his father's denouncers, the people Tony blamed, it wasn't long before he started threatening us."

"How?" Herb asked.

Roy clenched his jaw. "Mostly it was vague—that we'd be sorry. I thought at first it was just bluster and pain until our place at the lake burned.

"But how that got started could never be proved."

Roy brought his right hand, fingers splayed, up to his face, as though trying to rub away something repugnant. "Then it got more overt. Notes started arriving, with only a couple of words like, 'Your Daughter' or 'Think Safety' or, the last one before we left Florida: 'Amy. Love. Ha-ha!'"

"They came through the mail?" Gracie asked, knowing that would comprise a federal offense.

Linda nodded. "Some were; but others arrived in a variety of ways, like fastened to an SAR lapel pin left on a porch stand. Roy's been a member of the Sons of the American Revolution for many years, and has held a variety of offices in the organization.

"How Andrew got hold of Roy's pin is still a mystery, but it was definitely his! However, the engraved initials on the back, the 'LJC'—that's L for Leroy, then James Cantrell—had deep scratches across them, as though he—as though my husband was being—deleted!" She almost choked on that word.

Gracie could see Herb open the top right drawer of his desk and take something out. She drew in her breath sharply at seeing what it was, but knew it was hidden from the eyes of the other two. The officer asked, "Were there other ways in which he threatened you?"

Linda twisted around so she could look up at her husband, but waited for him to answer. "Yes, there was." One hand again rubbed down across his face. "He and his father used to like walking together along the beach when he was little, and they'd made a collection of seashells, especially mollusks, which won awards for Andrew in Boy Scouts then, later, even in college.

"That last note I mentioned, with the *Ha-ha*—that was left on our doorstep there in Florida, taped to a shell."

Herb's hand came up on top of the desk, Gooseberry's shell across his palm. "Did it look something like this?"

Gracie needed no vocalized answer to that—Linda began sobbing and Roy's face was frozen in shock. He finally managed, "Where—did you get that?"

Herb nodded toward Gracie, who understood she was to tell about Gooseberry's discovery—which she did. Roy demanded, "Was there a note with it?"

"Not by the time he brought it to me. Perhaps there might have been one—but is it possible he could have figured that the shell, itself, was all that was needed?"

There was a slow nod. A long, drawn-out sigh. "Yes, that's all that would have been needed. . . ."

# Six

GRACIE WONDERED ALOUD, "If your families were so close and did things together, why wouldn't Amy realize who Andrew was, or what he was up to?"

"Actually, our families didn't know one another very well, and besides, Amy was quite a bit younger than he," Roy admitted. "It was Tony and I who did things outside of business, anyway. Especially golf—and that reminds me of something else: Andrew was an excellent golfer, expecting—at least hoping—to become a pro.

"He graduated from college with a degree in golf—"

*I must have misunderstood.* "A degree in golf?" Gracie asked.

"It had some sort of more-official-sounding title, like golf management or administration or something. Anyway, he'd had many interviews and offers, but finally chose to stay there in Florida with one of those super-exclusive golf courses."

"Ah, then that might be a starting place, Herb," Gracie suggested.

"I agree." Herb cleared his throat as he picked up his pen again. "Can you give me the name and address of that course, Mr. Cantrell?"

He not only gave its name, but the location, and manager. However, "He's no longer there—which is another reason he hates me; he lost that position when it was discovered that his father frequently made up the foursome when the wealthy and famous played there.

"When the scandal broke, some of them testified that Tony used those hours to talk them into investing with him—with *us*. By then he was apparently taking bigger and bigger risks, and some of those golfers lost appreciable amounts.

"And were among the first to file for restitution!"

Gracie thought aloud: "That club would still have all the information in their files somewhere, wouldn't they? His full description, likes and dislikes, if and where he was competing in tournaments and if there was a particular chain of motels or hotels he stayed at when away? It might even tell where he's living, and could possibly say if he was married. . . ."

"He wasn't when we knew him," Linda put in. "He had many women, but marriage was not on his mind."

Gracie nodded to show she'd heard, but went on with what she hoped they might learn from a call. ". . . And they could send his picture electronically." But then she noticed the wall clock—and verified the time with her watch. The minutes were passing much too quickly!

"I'd like you to describe Andrew for me," Herb told them, "in as complete detail as possible."

They did so, their description much like that Gracie had received from Abe. The major difference, however, was that the Cantrells thought he must be around twenty-eight, perhaps even thirty. Linda frowned. "He always used to look young for his age, but we haven't seen him for a while. Intense hatred of that kind just could have eaten away his youthful appearance. . . ."

It was a severe shock to learn that not only had he followed them now to their new home, but that their daughter had been meeting Andrew Hively secretly. Linda fretted, "Maybe it was our fault for not having told Amy more, but she was just a child and all we wanted was to protect her. How could we have explained and not made her fearful?"

Gracie tried to make her feel a little better, "Even that might not have helped, though. We don't even know if Andrew was using his correct name."

". . . But that she'd go behind our backs—not tell us she had a new boy—er, man-friend!" Linda tilted her head around to look up at her husband again. "We thought we were sparing her, letting her make new friends in a new community, a new school, and a new church. And she seemed to be happy. . . ."

". . . And almost never mentioned Florida anymore," he finished for her.

Herb looked into the eyes of each of the three in turn. "If *you* were Amy and wanted to get out of ICU to meet someone, how might you go about it?"

There was a brief silence before Gracie suggested, "First of all, it wouldn't be enough to just get out of that unit. I'd first have to make contact with my friend, who'd apparently not been able to see me—if he even knew I was in intensive care. . . ."

"That's true," Herb agreed. "We don't know if they have friends in common—friends of hers from whom he could learn where she was."

". . . So I'd have to somehow call him, and in order to do that I'd need money for the pay phone in the hall, which I'd try to get from someone. And I couldn't be wearing a hospital gown to make that call, for any nurse or cleaning lady or anyone at the hospital would recognize from the color-coding that I belonged in ICU, right?"

He nodded, and she continued, "So—I'd have to be in 'civilian clothes' and wait for just the right moment, perhaps when some other patient needed the attention of the unit. If I left immediately when that happened, got out into the hallway and made a quick call to a number I'd memorized, I could keep going to someplace where he could pick me up."

"But why wouldn't she have told us. . . ." Linda began, then stopped. "But she's only seventeen and—and I guess . . . I guess that's the answer. Teens think no one understands."

Gracie placed a hand on her arm. "Look, it's not going to

do any good for any of us to blame ourselves—for anything. What's important is figuring out where she is."

"And if she's all right!" Roy himself seemed to have aged ten years in these last minutes. Linda used the arms of her chair to help push herself to her feet and into his arms, where they clung sadly to one another.

Gracie started to get up, too, wanting to go to them, to put her arms around them and offer her support, as well. But Herb must have realized that, and gave a tiny negative movement with his head, then a slight frown. "We've got people calling every motel and rooming house in the area, starting with Willow Bend and working out from here. I'll phone Florida right now," his finger touching the pad on which he'd written what the Cantrells had told him, "then get all additional information to those involved in the search."

He was standing, turning toward the open door, then back again. "Is there anything more you can tell me, anything at all that might help us identify him?"

"How I wish there were!" Linda cried, and the others grimly nodded agreement. She and her husband were almost to the back door when she added, "We'll go home and get some snapshots of Amy, recent ones, and bring them back here."

Gracie didn't want to look at her watch again—but couldn't keep from glancing at the big wall clock. In just a little over one hour the concert, the contest they'd been preparing so hard for, would begin at Waxmire Tabernacle, so she must get going soon!

♪

*However, God, I'd better check in with You again. That last answer of Yours was a doozy, if You don't mind my saying so— having me call the police station, and all. But is there anything else I should be attending to before going home for Uncle Miltie . . . ?*

She'd been driving back the same way she'd come, so was nearing Amy's again—which reminded her of Patsy Clayton waving at her, beckoning. *Well, if she's outside, Lord . . .* but she'd hardly thought that when she glanced to her right, and there she was, right there to the left of the sidewalk, at the beginning of the temporary ramp, which had been built for her convenience.

*She's such a plucky little thing, God. Just look at her there as she pushes the walker forward, using those front wheels, then setting down those nonskid hind feet, or whatever they're called, so it won't roll backward, then take a step forward. And another.* Gracie pulled to the curb and got out, but wasn't noticed by the child until the car door slammed.

She looked around, seeing Gracie hurrying across her lawn. Surprised, Patsy lost that rhythm she'd been using and, forgetting to press down on the rubber-tipped legs, realized in a moment that the walker was starting to roll backward.

She grabbed for the railing beside her just as Gracie came running to pull her close, safe against herself. "Oh, Patsy, I was so afraid you'd fall!"

She turned, her thin little arms around Gracie's waist, the binoculars hanging from a black band around the child's neck digging into her abdomen. "I was scared! Thanks for catching me."

"I'm afraid I distracted you." Gracie steadied her as she got back in position to use the walker. "I'm sorry I couldn't stay when I saw you before, but I had to be somewhere else right away."

"I figured that must be it." The child moved another slow step up the ramp. "And I'm glad you came back."

"I'm glad, too, Patsy, but I can't stay for more than a few minutes. This is the day we have the choir contest—do you know about that?"

"Um-hmmm. Amy was going to sing special parts, but now she can't, since she's in the hospital."

Gracie didn't think she'd better tell her that Amy was no longer there—she wouldn't have time to make detailed explanations. She was glad she'd kept silent when Patsy said, "That man was real worried when I told him she was there."

She sucked in a quick breath, but forced herself to speak calmly. "What man was worried, dear?"

"The nice man who brought her presents." But then she giggled. "But I'd rather have candy, or a toy, or a book."

*It can't be what I'm thinking of, but....* "What kind of presents did he bring her?"

"I—don't know about other times, but I saw him two times bring a big seashell. Isn't that a silly present?"

Gracie shivered, although the day was mild. "Maybe—Amy likes silly presents."

Patsy sobered. "Oh, I forgot; I should have told him she didn't get one of them. Gooseberry picked it up in his mouth from beside the front door and carried it away."

*Does Patsy spend all her time watching over there?* "What about the other one? Do you know if Amy got that?"

"I s'pose." She shrugged her thin shoulders. "But Mama called me for breakfast, so I didn't see who found it."

"So—both shells were brought early in the morning?"

"Not real early." She was finishing her slow advance up the slope. "Her dad goes to work early, before I get up; it's later when Amy and her mama leave for school. Did you know her mama gets to work with books all the time?"

"Yes, I understand she's a librarian there." She'd responded to the question, but her mind was much more on the fact that Amy may have found the shell first, before her mother could have. Or, was it possible that Gooseberry had made off with both of them on different mornings? It was not beyond him to have carried it some distance, then laid it down.

Like Uncle Miltie's screwdriver; they didn't find that for a week, not until, while clipping the thickly growing, cinnamon-colored chrysanthemums by the garage, he happened to see the handle sticking out from beneath the plants.

"Did the man leave notes with his presents?"

Her curly brown hair bounced with the shake of her head.

"He took the shell out of a bag—but I didn't see a paper."

"Did you talk with him more than that one time, when you told him she was in the hospital?" But then she heard someone approaching, and the screen door opened.

"Well, hel*lo*, Gracie," Marilyn Clayton exclaimed, stepping outside. "I thought I heard Patsy talking to someone, but didn't know who it was. Sit down and stay awhile."

"Thanks, but I can't this time. Patsy was outside as I drove by, and I just stopped to see how she's doing. I must get to the Waxmire Tabernacle for that choir concert this afternoon."

"Oh dear! What with everything else, that slipped my mind."

"Can we go, Mama?" the child urged.

"It will be all singing, Patsy—a bunch of choirs all singing the same thing. You don't really think you'd enjoy that, do you?"

Gracie laughed. "It's a little better than that. There is one 'required' piece—but we're allowed to make changes, so none of them will be exactly alike. And each of the churches also has the opportunity to choose its other number, which can be anything—so there's bound to be a variety."

"Can we go, Mama? *Can* we?"

Marilyn looked at her watch. "I—guess we can make it."

Gracie had also checked—and barely squelched a groan. "I've got to be there within the next half-hour, but you'd have at least forty-five minutes. And, as an added incentive, there will be delicious refreshments following the competition!"

"*Can* we?" Patsy was tugging at her mother's arm. "Please?"

"You do realize, dear, that if we go we won't leave until the concert's all over, right?" The young mother wanted to make sure of this.

"Right!" she repeated. "And I want to wear my new red jumper and the white blouse with the red flowers . . . !"

Well, there were now two more going to the concert—but Gracie couldn't help wondering if the very fact of its being such a glorious fall day might keep many away. *Now stop this, Gracie Lynn Parks, stop right this minute thinking in terms of the first year or two, when the attendance was so low.*

*It's been increasing each year—which is the reason Waxmire got to have another turn at hosting it, and we were skipped. I'd be happy if their huge auditorium is filled to overflowing . . . !*

*Dear God, please help us win at least something.*

She consciously corrected that last part, for she did know better than to pray so selfishly. *Okay, Lord, I know that each choir has worked really hard at making preparations for this, and we're all hoping to win. So just do, please, help us—help all of us to do our very best—and help the judges to do their best, too, and to judge with no prejudice as to size or position or anything other than our music and our presentations.*

She was still a minute or two from home when she looked around to make sure there was no traffic before calling on her cell phone to let Uncle Miltie know she'd be there in a few minutes, but would be leaving again right away. "Since I have my choir robe and music with me here in the car, I don't have to go back to our church."

"Good! But you do have a couple of phone calls."

"That shouldn't surprise me! But who were they—and must they be dealt with right away?"

"Well, not right away—except for Anna's. She wants to know if you can pick her up, to take her to Waxmire."

"Are you about ready to leave, Uncle Miltie?"

"I sure am."

"Then could you do me a favor? Call her back, and say we'll be there within ten minutes."

"Okeydokey—it's as good as done."

"Great!" But she had to ask, "Who were the other calls from?"

"Two are going to call back, but the other was from Estelle—and I told her you weren't here, but that you would definitely be at the concert, so she could talk with you there."

"Well done, Uncle Miltie. Keep this up and I'll have to double your salary!"

They both laughed; doubling zero was not about to make him a rich man.

Uncle Miltie had never seen the Tabernacle parking lot this full, and with another quarter-hour yet to go! Looking around, he exclaimed, "I'm sure glad we're no later. Many of the best seats must already be taken, and I'd hate having to climb up into the balcony—many of the best seats must already be taken."

But he led the way with his walker, and Anna, one hand on his shoulder and the other wielding her cane, walked slowly up the aisle with him. A number of attendees spoke to them, but finally they settled into the last aisle seats in the sixth row—with Rick's wife and daughter cheerfully moving to center seats to make room for them.

Uncle Miltie leaned over to whisper in Anna's ear, "Hey, there *are* advantages to being the halt and the blind."

And Anna laughed. "You're right, George Morgan. And it's good to be reminded of that. . . ."

❧

Gracie had seen them start down the aisle, and considered going with them, to make sure they found seats together, but one of the ushers assured her, "I'll keep an eye on 'em for you, Gracie. I know you're directing your choir, and I'll bet they're getting mighty nervous about you not being with them."

Seeing the twinkle in his eyes, she laughed. "I wouldn't be one bit surprised. So thanks," and she hurried to where all of her choir was already robed and standing around nervously.

"Where have you been?" Estelle demanded. "I called, and you weren't there, and your uncle wasn't sure where you were or when you'd get back."

"Oh, I had an errand to see about, then picked up someone who wanted to come hear us." Gracie was not about to get upset. "I understand my uncle assured you I'd be here on time, and I am."

She'd put on her robe while talking and now slid the stole over her head and patted the V-shaped front into its proper position, knowing that the longer "V" in the back would take care of itself.

When one member of the choir mentioned that she'd been too nervous to eat lunch, Don grinned. "Remember last year? I think these churches make a deliberate effort to outdo one another with all the goodies they prepare for us to eat after the singing. I don't doubt for a moment that we'll all make up for any starvation at lunchtime."

Then Rick turned to Paul, who'd just joined them. "And *you*, Pastor, plan on getting in on all the goodies afterward without even singing a note, don't you?"

"But of course!" The young minister laughed. "You couldn't possibly think I'd pass that up."

Several of the women appeared to be quite tense, but it was hard to tell with some; Tish and Tyne, not surprisingly, were whispering to each other. Gracie could see and appreciate the effort Barb was making to appear relaxed and carefree, and noted that it helped to draw her into some of the informality and fun the rest were having.

It was the responsibility of the host church, along with the choir directors, to arrange the seating of each choir. As the organist was playing and the five-minute-warning was given, everyone lined up in prearranged order, ready to march in, hymnals in hand, to sing along with the congregation.

Gracie always loved this—Willow Bend's finest singers, Willow Bend's saints from all the churches, all in one accord as they lifted their voices to "make a joyful noise together" while entering one of the sanctuaries of the Lord!

Her chest felt so full that for a moment she wondered if she really could sing at all, but then it was time for her alto voice to meld with all these others—and it was good. Very good! Whether Eternal Hope Community Church won or lost in the competition, she knew that every person here today had already won a wonderful reward—singing the praises of the Lord together.

There were many ahead of them, quite a few behind, and all were taking their seats in order, with no mix-ups. *Thank You, Lord. I don't think that You, either, would want any of these wonderful people to be embarrassed as they congregate here in this church today.*

Even as she sang, she'd glanced around. Back there on the left was Abe. And Rocky and his photographer were in the very front-center of the balcony. He gave her a thumbs-up, and she couldn't keep from smiling back at him. And there were Uncle Miltie and Anna, and oh, so many others she knew and loved!

As they finished singing, the host pastor came to the

podium, welcoming all who had come to bring their gift of singing, as well as those who had come to listen to and support them. There was Scripture and prayer—and then it was time for the first choir to come forward.

Their order had been chosen by lot—with the stipulation that no church would be in either the first or last position in consecutive years. So this year's opener was the Bethesda Methodist choir, an average-sized group of fifteen, which, with Amy not here, was the same size as Eternal Hope's.

Gracie listened attentively, for the excellent and for any less-than-perfect parts. She, as well as anyone else who was interested, had access to the scoring sheets that would be used by the judges, so she now tried to assess what she'd give this group had she been one of those who had to make this decision.

Yes, they were good—but Gracie didn't think they'd probably be among the winners. Next came the choir of the Trinity Episcopal Church; she knew some of these people as soloists, and their choice of music was wise for them—showcasing two of their superior voices, belonging to the physical education teacher from the high school and Suzie Frantz, who home-schooled her three children.

By the third and fourth choirs, however, she was already confused. *If I gave number one an eight on this part of the scoring, then maybe this one should be a nine—but on the other hand, on the next part I don't think this is quite as good, so. . . .*

By the fifth choir, from Evangelical Free, she gave up on

estimating possible scores and thanked God she wasn't a judge—from then on she settled back to enjoy to the fullest the rest of the program.

It was always a well-guarded secret right up until the bulletins were made as to what each church choir picked for its anthem-of-choice—and what a variety there was, far more than she'd guessed even when seeing those titles on the program! Of course that was to be expected: *We Sing of Hope*, turned out to be quite a jazzed-up rendering, while *Joy in the Morning* was comparatively subdued, dealing as it did with pain and heartbreak, yet getting through it with God's help. . . .

*How can the judges possibly give meaningful scores when comparing the rendition of a Medieval chant with a Spiritual? Or a moody, a cappella rendering of a nineteenth century English ballad with a modern rap-type, rhythmic chanting in unison?*

And then, at last, it was time for number six, Eternal Hope's presentation.

Barb walked to the organ, and as she played the first note they all arose. Yes! Everyone took the right position and processed exactly as done in church this morning. They approached the risers and those who could use help were given an unobtrusive hand—and Gracie knew that the others, also, must be missing Amy's presence right there in the middle of the front row.

As Gracie took her position, facing them from in front of the center aisle, the smile on her face was genuine, coming as naturally as her quick, close-to-the-chest thumbs-up before she looked at Barb and nodded.

They moved into their rendition of *Hallelujah, Save Us, Lord* perfectly. The solo parts went well—as flawless as the harmony! And the ending, that ending, which they'd changed so many times, even at the final rehearsal, was a worshipful and meaningful "Amen."

She looked toward Barb, and saw her beaming as she exchanged her sheet music for the piece they'd sung earlier in the day. The whole group must know that was the very best they'd ever sung their required number—and now were without doubt ready for *Help Me to See Thee, Lord*.

The beginning went well, the solo and duet portions were on target—and the ending equal to what they'd done in the morning service! Every member of the choir was beaming— they, too, knew they'd done their best, and that that best was very good.

They came back to their seats, only Tish nearly stumbling as she stepped down from the riser. Even that was probably not observed by most, however, as Lester was right there to steady her. She looked somewhat embarrassed, but proceeded the rest of the way without incident.

Gracie walked across in front of them to extend her hand to Barb, returning from the organ. "Wonderful! Absolutely fantastic, Barb!" she whispered as they sat down next to one another.

And Barb whispered back, "Thanks for making me go

through with this—and for all your help."

Gracie simply could not have stopped smiling had she tried—which she wasn't about to do. "Thanks be to God . . . !"

The next group went up. It was painful to hear them flub their timing at one place near the beginning, but the rest of their performance went well.

Actually, all of the groups were good, but Gracie was sure her own choir was better than at least some. *If only we can win second or third place—even an honorable mention would be a major encouragement, God!* But then, again, she realized this was not a "proper" prayer; every group here had the right to, and probably had prayed something similar to that.

So she rephrased—no, she changed that to, "Thank You, Lord, for being with us during all the practicing, and the altering, and the making-do we were involved with. Thank You for the courage to try this, and the strength to hang in there. . . ."

The very process of praying reminded her of the girl who would have been such an important part of today if only—if only what? *Where is she, God? Is Amy all right? Please, please take care of her—don't let anything bad happen to her.*

*She's still alive, isn't she? She must be so scared if he took her away—although maybe not. For if she left the hospital with him, as we're assuming, of her own volition, perhaps whatever he's told her made her trust him more than she does her parents.*

*Does she know who he is—or is this just some "romantic fling" as far as she's concerned? But why those shells, God? Was this to be a message to Amy, or to her parents? They believe it was meant as a threat, which only they would recognize. But might he have had her believe that for him they held a totally different significance? Perhaps "eternal love," or something like that?*

*I've never heard of any romantic notions such as that, but what do I know? Anything's possible.*

*Indeed, Lord! What do I know . . . ?*

She sighed, sitting there in the front row of this huge, practically new sanctuary, and consciously decided it was time to turn this whole mess with Amy over to God. *She* certainly had no sure answer to apply to a single one of the many questions she'd been asking. But God did!

She was a bit reluctant again to offer the other part of what she'd previously prayed, that God might act through her in any way He chose. He'd taken her up on her willingness before and, though Gracie was glad she'd obeyed, what now might be His call to action?

She started to close her eyes but, realizing she mustn't let anyone think she was bored or going to sleep, focused on the stole of the soprano in the middle of the front row of singers now up there—Presbyterians.

*Okay, God, I'm here again. I didn't want to confess my hesitancy—but that's dumb, isn't it? You already know my thoughts even before I recognize them as such, so I guess I wouldn't have to put this in words for Your sake.*

*But for mine, it is necessary. Once having made the offer, I can't weasel out of it, telling myself I didn't understand the possible consequences. So here we go again—I'm willing, even if not as eager as I should be, to serve as Your hands and feet and mouth....*

# Seven

**G**RACIE HAD HALF-EXPECTED to be zapped with some earth-changing thought or message almost immediately—and was relieved that didn't happen.

At least now, having already made the commitment, she could just sit back and enjoy the rest of the concert—which wouldn't take much more time, seeing that the last choir, which happened to be Waxmire's, was now on the platform.

The organist, on his home-church instrument, was superb, and Gracie thought that he, alone, could so entrance the listeners (and the judges?) that they'd be tempted to give megapoints on that! But the choir, also, had a number of trained voices, especially Roberta Bennett and Chuck DeLancy. Both numbers appeared to be flawless, their music-of-choice being contemporary, with sections of definitely rap quality, with rhythmic chanting, often in unison.

*Well, I can't fault the judges if this church proves to be the winner—yet I'm almost hoping it isn't. With their getting first prize year before last, and a third last year, some of our smaller choirs may decide not to even try again.* She tried to search her mind to see if that was the real reason she hoped this—and thought it was.

The competition was finally over, and Dr. Kenneth Ebersoll, Waxmire's pastor, commended and thanked everyone who had participated and the many who'd come to hear this marvelous concert. He asked everyone to rise and join in singing all verses of *Amazing Grace* while the judges finished calculating the scores.

And then it was time for the announcement of the winners, also being done by Dr. Ebersoll, who first wished to state, on behalf of the judges, that this had been a remarkably close contest. "Three of the four winners to be announced are separated by less than thirty points out of the maximum of four hundred, or one hundred from each of the four judges.

"I shall in just a moment be announcing those winners, and ask that one member of that choir come forward to receive its award. I'll be starting with an honorable mention, then third, second, and first.

"We understand that you will want to applaud, but are asking that, as hard as this may be, you wait until the end, then clap to your hearts' content—applaud these four church choirs, but also *all* those you heard today, for every single group here is a winner."

Heightening the dramatic tension, the organist achieved a most satisfactory drumroll, and the pastor tore open a large, off-white envelope and brought out a matching document. "For the position of honorable mention, I have the privilege of announcing—Trinity Episcopal Church!"

Their music director came forward and accepted for the choir, all the while accompanied by another very l-o-n-g drumroll.

*Well, perhaps we'll be third,* Gracie thought, but with another drumroll, Dr. Ebersoll announced that this award was going to the Evangelical Free Church on the edge of town. It was only the second time this choir had joined the competition, and Gracie tried to be generous in thinking that recognition would be especially appreciated.

She found herself wriggling a little, and sat up straighter. She knew she couldn't keep from being at least a little biased, but it did seem to her that Eternal Hope just might rank up here somewhere. But the drumroll this time, signaling second place, was for—and she could hardly wait for the intentionally delayed announcement—Waxmire Tabernacle!

Gracie wiped her forehead, aware that she was actually perspiring. There was only one slot above Waxmire's—and four below Honorable Mention. Did she have the assurance—or the pride—to believe that, though they'd done as well as they ever had, they'd been able to top Waxmire?

It now had to be either first prize or nothing. And the

answer was already in that envelope, which Ken Ebersoll was opening so very, very slowly. Then the announcement: "And the first prize winner is . . . *Eternal Hope Community Church*!"

After church this morning, Barb offered to let Gracie go forward to collect their award, if they won one—but Gracie had insisted she was just one of the choir members, one who'd already been blessed by having had the opportunity to help with the directing this year.

Even as Barb went for the foot-high statuette of four singers, two men and two women, Dr. Ebersoll spread his arms and, with partially bent elbows, brought his hands within ten or twelve inches of one another and raised them, palms-upward. The people rose to their feet, and he was leading the applause, which went on and on.

Rick, beside Gracie, slipped a folded handkerchief into her hand—which was the first she realized that tears of unadulterated happiness were running down her cheeks. She put the white cotton square to good use, even while apologizing for needing it.

"Never has my handkerchief been so blessed." Rick was grinning. "What an occasion!"

Lester was hugging Barb, and the Turner twins were actually jumping up and down and laughing out loud!

When Ken again raised his arms, the applause finally died down and he reminded everyone of the invitation printed in the program, "Come on back to the social hall and join us for a time of fellowship and for snacks. What a wonderful day this has been; let's extend our time together!" And with that he gave the benediction.

Although there was a steady stream of people heading for the very large area behind the sanctuary, most choir members made their way more slowly than the others. Gracie, who'd lived in Willow Bend most of her life, was amazed at how many people she *didn't* know who said hello, or offered congratulations. Some were familiar-looking and she was sure they were from the general area, though she couldn't exactly place them.

She waved to friends who, deciding not to wait to speak with her now, were heading for the back; she hoped she'd see them there. She became aware of some of these relatives and friends of singers, who'd come from Ohio, Michigan, Illinois, and other states.

One Pennsylvanian commented about how rare such an ecumenical event was, and Gracie was pleased to share with her some of the other joint projects and services of this ministerium.

"That's wonderful," the woman approved, then added, "And now you can rest on your laurels until next year's competition."

She shook her head. "Oh, no, there's no resting yet. Waxmire and Eternal Hope now have the opportunity to go on to a regional event."

"Have you done that before?"

"*I* haven't—but this is the year...."

She'd finally started to head for the back room, wanting to have the chance to speak to Paul before he left, but was still being stopped repeatedly by well-wishers. Yet, with the contest behind her, she now needed to seize the opportunity to tell him of Amy's disappearance. She finally excused herself, promising several people that she'd see them later.

Paul was near the outside door by the time she finally got to this room. Looking around, she saw that Uncle Miltie and Anna were thoroughly enjoying themselves—but then, as she again started toward where her pastor had been, she could no longer see him. She got to the back door as quickly as possible, in time to see him step into his car halfway across the large parking lot.

Rushing out, she started to run diagonally across the large macadamed area, toward the exit. *Oh, God, please let him see me and stop! If only I were wearing my sneakers, like usual—I can't go any faster in these stupid heels....*

And yes! He did glance in her direction and stop, rolling down his window. "Gracie! Are you okay?"

Her hand reached to brace herself against his car. "I—I have to talk with you, Paul—before you leave...."

"What a day, Gracie!" He sounded exuberant. "I'm so proud of all of you!"

"I'm proud of them too. We did have some problems along the way, but every single person really came through."

"They—and *you* certainly did."

But she had to give him her message. "Paul, what I need to tell you is that Amy's no longer in ICU. . . ."

"Great! I was just heading over there to see her."

"But it's—not great, not at all!" She was panting, so drew in a big breath before explaining, "She somehow got away from the hospital during mid-to-late morning, and the reason I was late getting to the church this afternoon is that her parents and I were at the police station."

*"What?"*

He sounded as shocked as she'd been. "No one apparently knows anything for sure. She'd coaxed her mother to bring in 'civilian' clothing, sweat pants and tops, and also to leave her some quarters—so we're guessing she called the guy in the gray car. And that she's with him now."

"You—met with Herb?"

She nodded, still breathless. "They've traced the ownership of the car and it's registered to the son of an ex-partner of Roy's who committed suicide after his embezzlements were discovered. The son, Andrew Hively, sounds as though he has a serious mental problem—at least an all-consuming hatred for Roy, which may not bode well for Amy."

"So—what can we do?"

"I'm not sure there's much any of us can do. Except to pray—pray a lot!"

They each had many questions, but their attempts at making sense of such extraordinary events fell flat. The conversation couldn't have lasted more than a few minutes before

Gracie remembered to tell him, "We think it's best not to talk to anyone else about this right now—though I'm going back in to speak privately with Abe, if I can, since he's already involved."

"Thanks, Gracie, for doing all this. I'd have assumed she was much better had I gone to the hospital and they told me she'd left." He pressed his arms out against the steering wheel, pushing himself back into his seat. "What do you think about my going to see her parents?" His face was lined with uncharacteristic tension.

She hesitated. "I suppose that's a good idea—though I don't want them to think I'm going around talking about the situation. So, when you see them, please explain my coming to you."

As she went back inside and walked around visiting with people, she was suddenly startled when Rick asked if she'd brought the shell with her, so startled that she spilled some of her hot spiced cider. This mishap, however, did give her something to do while figuring out how to respond.

As she wiped up the liquid with her paper napkin, she simply said that she'd neglected to bring it—and she didn't think it was too important to know just what it was, anyway. Unfortunately, she didn't get away with that, for Uncle Miltie was nearby and stated that he most certainly did want it identified. "Where is it, Gracie?"

She avoided answering that by speaking to Anna, mentioning to her friend about having carelessly spilled her drink. "And it was so good. This early cider is the best of the year, isn't it?"

"I certainly enjoy it the most—but I've never been sure if that's because it's best, or if I'm so thirsty for it that it seems especially delicious."

And that led to Anna, Uncle Miltie, and several others talking about gathering apples of all kinds in the past, including macintosh, winesap, and smokehouse, and taking them to a family-run cider press. There were also remembrances of neighbors getting together and having a party with everyone working at making big copper cauldrons of apple butter, which was then shared by all.

From that moment on, Gracie made every effort to keep her distance from Rick and his curiosity, hoping he wouldn't again bring up the subject of that marine specimen she'd last seen being removed from Herb's desk drawer. She even wondered, now, if it would have been worthwhile, even possible, to check it for fingerprints.

She decided that would have been difficult, what with Gooseberry carrying it in his mouth, and Gracie and Uncle Miltie handling it, then Herb—and who knew how many others?

Herb! She'd better soon tell him what Patsy said about there being a second shell.

She'd seen Abe earlier across the crowd, but now she turned as a hand was placed upon her arm. "Oh, Abe, I'm so glad you came!"

"I'm glad too, Gracie. And I want you to know that I think you did a masterful job with your directing—especially on such short notice."

"Barb had it well under way before I sort of took over."

He was only two or three inches taller than Gracie, so with her wearing those unaccustomed heels, they looked straight into one another's eyes. "But you are very different people, with different talents, my dear Gracie. You are the optimist, the one who can help them see their capabilities and their strengths.

"They were not only singing for the contest today, they were singing for you."

She was flattered. "What I was hoping for was that they were singing for God."

"That too, Gracie." He grinned. "That too."

She reached for his cup. "Could I fill it with hot coffee?"

"That's not necessary. . . ."

"For me it is. How often have you refilled my cup of tea as I've sat in your deli and taken up your time with my problems—and the problems of those I love?"

"I'm not counting. For true friends, such times are always never enough."

She saw the warmth in his eyes. "I treasure our visits, also, Abe. And I may come to see you in the morning."

His hand had remained where he'd laid it, and now she felt a gentle tug as he nodded toward a table across the room. "I would like that, but perhaps now is the time to talk?"

She nodded, and took a step or two in that direction before stopping. "I just offered you a refill, and am now heading the other way. . . ."

"Better a refill of friendship than of coffee, Gracie."

"I'll second that." But they didn't exchange another word until they were seated.

"Our dear little Amy is missing," she said somberly.

His dark eyes widened, but he waited for her to continue. "She left intensive care without anyone seeing her. . . ."

"How did she manage *that*?"

"We have theories, not facts—as is true of almost everything connected with this case." A twitch of the corner of his mouth alerted her to having used that last word. "And don't you dare tease me about reading mystery novels!"

"I can't, not really. I, too, read mysteries."

She cocked her head. "You know, Abe, I thought I knew you very well, but we must never have got on that topic. Isn't that strange?"

"Not strange at all. Each of us has many facets, so many likes and interests that we wouldn't get bored even with conversations each day." But then the smile disappeared as he asked, "Do you have any idea where Amy could have gone?"

She shook her head. "Nor do we know the whereabouts of Andrew Hively, the owner of the gray car. But we suspect that when we find one, we'll find the other."

"This is not like the Amy I knew. She'd have to realize how terrible her family must feel, and how they'd worry. As well as her friends." He was frowning. "What would make a girl like Amy run away?"

"I don't know." Her gaze seemed fixed upon the reflected gleam of a big electric coffeepot, but she wasn't actually seeing it. "That's what makes this so hard. To the best of my knowledge, she got along well with her parents—that is, as well as a normal seventeen-year-old of today will let herself get along with them."

But then she wondered aloud, "Did she ever tell you why she was working? Why she wanted or needed the money?"

"Not really. When she first came to see me she indicated that she wanted to work as many hours as possible, and I asked if she was working toward something. What she mentioned was education, and possibly, sometime in the future, a car.

"But she never seemed to spend money on herself. The clothes she wore were all right, but she didn't appear to have a large wardrobe—not like I see with other girls her age—or think I see." He shook his head. "But I was not blessed with a daughter, so perhaps I do not have the clearest vision where teenaged girls are concerned."

"I suspect you see more clearly than you know, my friend." She shifted position. "Apparently there have been serious money problems in that household."

"Yet both parents are employed, and neither is in a minimum-wage position—they're far above that."

"I—don't know just how bad things are in that regard, whether they still owe a lot of money, or anything like that.

But I did notice that her mother wears no jewelry, not even a wedding ring—so I suppose that's a possibility."

"Which could account for many things. . . ."

It was then that Uncle Miltie came over to them, teasing. "Talk about being stuck-up, Gracie Parks! You direct a choir that wins this year's trophy, then hide out over here in the corner!"

She reached to lay her hand on his, on the walker. "It's been a very big day, and I've talked with an awful lot of people. It's a relief just to sit here with a good friend and quietly visit."

"Well, I'm not trying to rush you or anything, but thought I'd let you know that if you were staying because of Anna and me, we're ready whenever you say the word."

She pushed back from the table. "Frankly, Uncle Miltie, I'm bushed. I'd appreciate going home and relaxing."

Abe got to his feet first, and reached to help her up. "I hope you will have a calm, quiet evening and get a good night's rest."

"Thanks, Abe. I do need that."

"I'm sure you do. . . ."

∽

Uncle Miltie, though professing to be stuffed, still was willing to consider the possibility of a dish of ice cream later. After he shared that with Gracie, he headed for the living room TV set and settled into his recliner.

As soon as he was engrossed with what was on the screen,

Gracie phoned the police station, leaving a message for Herb, who was away from his desk, to call back. In the meantime, Marge dropped in, excited at the choir's success and not noticing her friend's distraction.

"Hi, Herb," Gracie said with relief, when he finally rang her, moments after her neighbor had left. "Anything new— that you dare tell me?"

"Not much, not for sure, anyway. How about with you?"

"Well, I'm not certain this is important, but did you have any idea that more than one shell was involved?"

"*More* than one?" He paused, though obviously interested. "Involved in what way?"

She filled him in on what Patsy had said, and realized she should have asked more questions. "I don't know if she spoke with him more than that once—and I hope the binoculars hanging from a cord around her neck won't make him skittish. Is it possible he might fear she saw too much?"

"Who knows?" Even over the phone, she could sense the coiled anxiety behind the police officer's caution.

"May I ask if you've been able to find out where he is, or was staying? Or anything about his recent activities?"

"We know where he was staying for a couple of nights— and he's been there other times, as well. But he's not there now. We also know he received one call prior to leaving, but not who it was from."

"Isn't it possible for phone records to show that and also outgoing messages from the phone outside of ICU?"

"Good suggestions, Gracie. And, yes, we're waiting for callbacks as to those. In the meantime, maybe you could check again with the child—Patsy, you said?"

"Um-hmmm. Patsy Clayton. She's been disabled all her life, and is now recovering from another orthopedic surgery, getting around with a walker." She didn't want to even think about the possibilities concerning her safety. "Herb, you don't think she could be in danger, do you? I don't need to tell her parents anything about what's going on, do I?"

She heard his deep intake of breath and subsequent release in a drawn-out sigh. "I wouldn't think so, Gracie—but reading about abnormal psychology and watching it in action are two very different things, so I wouldn't dare give an unequivocal, no."

"Then I'm going over there right away. I'm already so upset about Amy; if anything happens to Patsy, too, I—won't be able to live with myself!"

"Gracie . . . ?"

She was blotting away a tear. "What?"

"I don't think she's in danger, but I do think you've made the right decision here. Still, I *never* again want you to say that you won't be able to live with yourself!" It was only a split second later that his voice added, so softly she could hardly hear it, ". . . Although I do know, only too well, how easy it is to feel that way."

Her own voice became a little stronger. "Thanks, Herb. . . ." And she meant it.

Uncle Miltie was so involved with his program that she wasn't sure he'd even remember that she told him where she was going. Instead of walking, she decided to drive the familiar route in case she should need to go somewhere else afterward.

Just as she was heading up the walk to the Claytons, Linda Cantrell burst out of her front door, having spotted Gracie. She was obviously upset as she demanded, "Have you heard anything yet about Amy?"

"Not yet, dear." She spoke as gently as possible. "I was hoping that perhaps you had."

"Well, we haven't." She stood there wringing her hands, face showing her strain. "And I think it's time to call the radio and TV stations, so people know about our daughter's being kidnapped."

"We don't know that she has been, Linda." Gracie was trying to keep her voice calm and reasonable. "She's the one who voluntarily left the unit."

"But Amy would have come home." Her voice grew louder, as though volume alone could make her words true. "I know she would have—she probably expected him to bring her here, and he didn't!"

There was no point in arguing what would not, under the circumstances, probably have taken place. And Gracie didn't feel free to tell her that the police had determined where Andrew had stayed prior to receiving that phone call. "Do you keep close tabs on her friends and acquaintances?"

Her head moved slowly from side to side. "Not too much—not recently. We did at first, though. Then we seriously considered Andrew's threats. But it's been five years now—why would he wait for five whole years to make a move? To kidnap our Amy?"

Gracie would have had an answer to that had it been Herb or Abe asking, but she couldn't say to this distraught mother that the man could very well be mentally ill— that his continuing hatred could have finally pushed him over the edge of sanity. "I don't know. Could he possibly have been in prison? Or institutionalized?" She wished she'd thought to find out about this from Herb. They must have considered such a thing and checked it out.

Linda asked more questions, and then Roy emerged from their house to join them. By then, Gracie wasn't too surprised to have Patsy's mother and father appear at their door, looking out to see what was happening. *This is like old home week—or a movie-of-the week when the writer doesn't want someone to tell someone else something.*

But this was real life, and she chided herself for making that analogy. Besides, she had no way of knowing whether or not the Claytons even knew what the Cantrells were going through.

It turned out that all they knew was that Amy had been in

the hospital. When Roy and Linda, arms around one another, had returned to their house, Gracie casually attempted to learn if Patsy had told her parents about the man in the gray car.

But her calm tone didn't fool them. "Why didn't you tell us, Gracie? How *dare* you not let us know about this, so we could protect her?" They were now nearly as agitated as the Cantrells.

"That's why I'm here," she tried to explain.

"That was hours ago when you talked with Patsy. Anything could have taken place during that time and it would all have been your fault!"

How could she respond to that? A little matter of getting to the church on time—a minor thing like winning first place in the competition paled in significance against a mother and father's possible loss of their daughter.

She was still attempting to get in a few words when an unmarked black car pulled up and Herb, in casual clothing— jeans and plain navy sweatshirt—got out and strode toward them.

Gracie introduced them, learning that the Claytons and Herb knew one another by sight, but little more. It was the police officer who asked, "Do you suppose we could go up on the porch or into the house instead of standing out here?"

That was one thing, at least, on which they could all agree, so they entered the house and went into the living room. In the next room, where Patsy was sitting in her wheelchair, the television was on, but Gracie decided not to interrupt, stopping only to wave and smile at her young friend before settling herself with the other adults. Looking around, she waited for Herb to take the lead.

He asked first how long she'd been here and, learning it had been only a few minutes, said, "Then I guess we'd better start from the beginning."

He ran through the facts he knew and was willing to share with the Claytons: Amy's leaving ICU, the shell found by Gooseberry, and, most importantly, Patsy's account of the second shell left next door. "Did either of you see this second one?"

When they replied in the negative, he asked permission to invite their neighbors back, to continue the exchange of information.

Linda and Roy, both stiff with anxiety, walked in, confirming they'd seen neither of the shells until he'd shown them that first one at his office. And it was difficult enough for Patsy's mother to believe her daughter had seen one mysterious shell, let alone an additional one. Perhaps Patsy had merely seen the same one on two different occasions, or got her days mixed up.

But when she learned that her little girl had not only spoken with the suspect, but had innocently informed him that Amy was in the hospital, she grew even more upset.

Again Gracie was under fire—"You should have told us! It would have been your fault had she been kidnapped, too— had she had something horrible happen to her. . . ."

# Eight

AS HERB TRIED TO CALM Patsy's mother, Gracie realized to what extent she'd been caught in the middle; from now on, she'd better check back with him before snooping independently.

It was certainly obvious that neither set of parents thought much of the way she'd handled things!

To defuse the situation, Herb asked for help in suggesting theories as to what could have taken place—even knowing that some of these would quickly be proven unlikely, or shot down right away.

Speculation one, that Andrew had only just now located the Cantrells and, discovering that Amy was in the hospital, decided immediately to make his move, was discarded since he had been "dating" her—or at least seeing her off and on for at least a couple of months.

Speculation two, suggested by Roy, fared little better: Amy, either on her way to the rehearsal or after her arrival, had eaten or drunk something that made her ill. (Better, of course, would be if she had just contracted some fast-acting virus.) Then, after she'd been taken to the hospital, Patsy told the strange man where she was, and he somehow managed to sneak in and see her there, talking her into getting out and leaving with him.

Linda insisted that her Amy had too much sense, and that she loved them too much to do something like that, especially when she knew how worried they were about her. Besides, she was much too weak, just recovering . . . and she began to cry.

Roy tried to comfort her, and other scenarios were mentioned, none of them answering all the questions they had. Herb put in quietly, "These are all suppositions based on her knowing who he really is. Suppose for a bit that he might have used an alias. . . ."

"Why should he?" Roy demanded. "I'm sure he wanted us to know—to worry and suffer. And how do we know he wasn't the one who gave her whatever it was that made her so sick so quickly."

Linda Cantrell groaned, putting her hands to her face in horror. "How much more we'd suffer if everything could be kept hidden until he'd accomplished—whatever he had in mind to do. . . ."

Gracie murmured, "Perhaps he didn't know how much she'd been told, what she knew. Is it possible he started out

just feeling his way—and discovered she was truly a trust-
ing young girl who hadn't yet lost her faith in other people?

"Maybe it took him this long to—to poison her mind
against her parents—to make her choose him over you.
Couldn't that be his ultimate revenge?"

By now, Linda was holding on to her husband's arm, as if
to keep from drowning. "I can't stand this, Roy—this not
knowing...."

Nobody had the heart to remind her that she had no
alternative.

"You've still not located the car?" Gracie asked.

Herb's eyes flickered slightly, as though he was unclear as
to what he should answer, how much they ought to know.
After a moment of hesitation, he said, "Yes, Gracie, we did
find the car, in a Chicago suburb, but...."

"Then where's Amy?" Linda strained at the edge of her
seat. "She's all right, isn't she?"

"... We don't know where either of them is. We're checking every motel and hotel in the whole area, as well as car
rental and public transportation places."

"Then isn't it time to call in the experts?" her father
demanded. "If he's taken her across state lines—and she *is*
still a minor, you know—this is an FBI matter, right?"

Linda reminded them, "I've been wanting to call the TV
stations, get her picture out there all over the place, so someone who's seen her will call!"

"And yet," Herb continued, still speaking in the same controlled voice, "supposing there's too much publicity and he becomes scared, afraid she will be recognized. Can he then keep her hidden? Or will he feel forced to . . . ?" He left that sentence unfinished.

The room all at once seemed airless and silent, quiet enough for Gracie to become aware of the music from the Disney tape Patsy was watching in the next room. It was the delightful tune sung by the Seven Dwarfs as they whistled their way home from work—its mood of cheer utterly incongruous with this room's atmosphere.

"May I propose that we let the law continue doing things its way for at least another twenty-four hours?" Gracie offered.

Linda glared at her. "The law has let that man take my daughter out of the state already. We don't know how she is or what he's doing to her . . . !"

Herb put in, "I sympathize with your wanting to take quick action, Mrs. Cantrell, but we don't even know if Amy is with him. If she is, then this man's mental state. . . ."

"He's a horrible man, a kidnapper, and—he's already threatened us, frightened us—we don't know what he's capable of!" She paused no longer than it took for a quick breath. "I *am* going to call the TV networks!" And she jumped up from where she'd been sitting beside her husband on the couch.

"Mrs. Cantrell!" Herb's voice was firm, commanding, the first time Gracie had heard that tone from him. "Be seated!"

Linda was so startled that she actually did what he told her. He was still seated in his chair, both feet flat on the floor and with no evident movement having taken place, but he now looked, even out of uniform, like someone to be obeyed.

His gaze stayed on her. "I haven't wanted to say this to you, not wanting to worry you more, but the reason you've heard nothing from or of Andrew Hively for five years is that he's been institutionalized in Florida. . . ."

She stared at him, eyes huge; it was her husband who demanded, "What kind of institution?"

"A mental hospital. Had you kept up your ties back there, you'd undoubtedly have heard that he'd, in fact, been doing many peculiar, even destructive things. He'd been arrested and finally was going to trial when his lawyer appealed to the court, necessitating a series of psychological evaluations.

"The result: He was determined to be unfit for trial."

Gracie knew to ask anything else might prove even more traumatizing for the Cantrells. Still, there was a real chance the answer might make things better. "Herb, would it help us to know what *kind* of strange and harmful things Andrew had been doing? Did he become a danger to people, or just property? Was he ever threatening or harming any women?"

He shook his head. "Not that we know of—not as far as I could find out. One of his earliest episodes involved his going up and down a rural road, in the middle of the day, shooting the connections—the insulators—off electric poles. Another came to light when perfect strangers began reporting calls from him, in which he insisted they were close family friends, and left really weird messages, like the date and time on which their deaths would occur—always within ten days!

"Also, he'd start out with a bucket of paint and a brush, covering with huge, brush-wide smears of brilliant red paint every bit of graffiti he could find. . . ."

"There was nothing—aggressive? No actual physical assault against anyone?"

"Again, not that we know of. That's not to say it's an impossibility."

Gracie felt it was time to ask, "So what do you think the odds are, Herb, that he might have her with him for—well, just for company? That he's obsessive but not really violent?" She could sense the Cantrells stiffening with fear as they awaited Herb's reply.

"I'd never hazard a guess like that, Gracie! Not ever! There are too many personal variables, and situational ones to allow me to figure out what will happen." He glanced around the group before again focusing on Gracie. "I, personally, have been doing a whale of a lot of praying for her and for all of you—and suggest you do likewise."

He pushed himself up by pressing down on the arms of his chair. "I'm leaving now. I was officially off today, but I have been on during the night and since mid-morning. You can leave any messages on the station answering machine. I'll check them at least every hour, because I'm also expecting answers to several different queries. . . ."

Gracie realized how exhausted he was—and would have liked to leave when he did. But Patsy had let her know she'd like company for the end of *Snow White*, and Gracie wanted to keep things as normal as possible for her in the midst of this stressful situation, which Patsy thus far was not aware of. Gracie knew that the two couples were still in the front room talking, and was relieved when, a short time later, she heard the Cantrells depart.

As the credits began to roll, she chatted with the child about the story and characters and asked, "Don't you think Snow White should have known better than to eat that apple?"

Patsy considered for a moment, then said, "Well, I'd maybe have liked to just taste it, 'cause it was sure a beautiful apple, and I. . . ."

"Patsy! Don't *ever* eat things given to you by strangers!" Her mother had entered the room just in time to hear that reply, and was clearly agitated. "That may be why Amy was so sick—maybe someone gave her something bad."

"I know, mama. You've always told me, but why—would Amy do that? Didn't her mama tell her not to?" she asked, wide-eyed.

Mrs. Clayton threw up her hands. "I don't know what

other mothers tell their children, but you know I want you to be careful. That's what's most important."

The child nodded. "All right. I'll only eat it if I know the person who gives it to me."

Her mother again left the room, and Gracie wished she could add to that. She had the feeling that Amy would not have taken anything from someone she didn't know, either, but by this time she did know Andrew—or whatever he might have called himself—very well.

*If* he gave her something to eat or drink, she would probably have consumed it. What reason would she have to suspect him of wanting to harm her?

Uncle Miltie reported that he'd just answered a call on the fourth ring, and was sure the line was open, but no one spoke. "I've been promising myself to buy one of those gizmos that automatically records the phone number of all callers, and I'm definitely going to get one tomorrow morning!" she informed him. But now she was going to take a shower and head for bed. She needed it!

Another call came while she was in the bathroom—but once again there was no answer when her uncle picked up the receiver. Could this be a form of harassment? Or was it someone who wanted to speak only to her?

Could Amy be trying to reach her? That possibility kept her tossing and turning a long time before she went to sleep.

How she hoped that, if that was the case, Amy would do it again. And talk to her. *Please, Lord, be with Amy and her family and friends. Even if she deliberately left with Andrew, even if for some reason she's angry with us or wants nothing to do with us in the future. If Amy is still alive, God, please get her in touch with someone here.*

There were no more calls throughout the night.

Gracie awoke even earlier than usual, her first thoughts on the missing girl. Picking up the Bible from beside her bed, she held the soft-bound volume between her palms, riffling through the pages with her right thumb. She knew the words, and said them to herself—yet had to see them printed, had to read them.

Near the end of *Matthew*. After the resurrection. Jesus there in Galilee with His disciples, about to leave in that physical form of His strong, earthly manhood in which they all knew Him so well. He was giving them the Great Commission— they were to tell everyone the good news of His being the Messiah. It was the message meant for not only those throughout the then-known world, but throughout the entire world.

Yes, here it was, at the very ending of Matthew's account: *Lo, I am with you always, even unto the end of the world.*

She lay there looking at those words, reading them again, and praying. She'd been praying all along that Amy would not be too frightened, but now Gracie qualified that. *Please* help her to recognize if she's in danger, and give her the opportunity to get word to me—or to someone else who can be of more assistance than I know how to be.

Only You, Lord, know if notifying the media would make things worse for Amy—if so, please don't let her mother do that. And that goes for all of us, me, too—help us to do only what will make things better. I hope my going to Abe and to her parents and their neighbors is what I was supposed to do—it seemed right, but how am I to know?

Please do let me know what to do, Lord.

She was reminded of their anthem yesterday, Help Me to See Thee, Lord. Yes, that was so very fitting right now, so apropos. Even in a mess like this one, You are here. But I so often don't look for You, or pay attention to what You're doing. Help me, Jesus, to see You in everything and everyone I see today.

She got out of bed and went to the window. There were glimmerings of morning light, enough for her to fit in her walk before starting her day, with all the surprises it might hold. She smiled, remembering Elmo's comment about going five days a week to his business, while Gracie kept involved with her busyness seven full days and then some.

The last thing she did before leaving the house was to take the phone off its hook and lay it on the stand; she wanted to be there should there be more calls.

She was still thinking of her husband as she and Gooseberry started off for their walk. Oh, El, I miss you so terribly. What I wouldn't give to have you here beside me, to hold me *and help me and BE me. I never fully appreciated until we were married what was meant when at weddings, especially, there was the emphasis on "two becoming one."*

*But we were. We really were—which is why sometimes I now feel so incomplete. How I wish I could talk things over with You, like now with this Amy problem. You had so much common sense—not just book learning, though you did have that—but wisdom. And you had so much patience, in so many ways. . . .*

She kept on walking, ignoring Gooseberry, who was sometimes underfoot but more often wandering around checking under bushes, around fences, even under parked cars in driveways. She was confident after all their walks together that he knew better than to go out into the street.

When they got as far as the Cantrells, it seemed to her as if he was giving this property a more thorough examination than most. She couldn't help but wonder if he was hoping to find another shell.

They walked on to the police station, where Gracie learned that Herb should be arriving within a few minutes. Feeling unusually restless, she told the woman on the desk that she'd walk around another block or two before coming back. She got only as far as the sidewalk when he arrived.

He had learned nothing more overnight. She figured it was worth mentioning all those "message-less" calls at her home, and told him she intended to buy, as soon as the stores opened this morning, one of those machines to record phone numbers of incoming callers.

"That's wise, particularly under these circumstances," he told her. "I've had one for a long time—and it's certainly good for cutting down on crank calls."

"I—hadn't realized. . . ."

He looked at her. "You're learning about all the cranks and crazies out there, aren't you, Gracie."

She looked up at him, this handsome, strong, wise man, this public servant she'd so taken for granted, not even wondering what his work—his life must be like. "How do you stand it, Herb?"

The crooked grin he'd flashed her was gone, but now a slow smile, more sad than happy, took its place. "I love this town and its people. If I didn't, I wouldn't still be here."

Gracie found she couldn't speak right then, and he added, "And, like you, dear friend, I try to help matters out by praying."

Gracie had asked Uncle Miltie to leave the phone's receiver lying where it was until after she'd come back from the store. But it wasn't long before he was able to tell her, on her return: "That's it, Gracie. Your new device is connected and should be operational."

He looked at her for approval, and his niece gave him an immediate hug. "Thanks for taking care of this for me."

"For *us*," he corrected. "I don't enjoy this kind of shenanigan any more than you do!"

They ate breakfast together, and he went outside to check on his flowers. Gracie was restless and worried and found herself moving around aimlessly. In an effort to distract herself—more important than the fact that the last ginger cookie had been eaten—she decided to make up a batch of snickerdoodles.

This cookie recipe had been handed down for generations— at least back to her great grandmother, possibly before that—and she hardly needed to look at the somewhat yellowed card on which the ingredients were so carefully handwritten.

She smiled, remembering her daughter-in-law wanting to copy it and many other old favorites on her last visit, and asking about this one, "How do you know how much flour to add, Mom?"

"Doesn't it say?"

"'Use enough flour to stiffen' is what's written here, but. . . ."

Gracie laughed. "I'm afraid you'll find that on many of the old recipes, dear. Those earlier cooks didn't have the measuring equipment that we're familiar with and use today, and their flour wasn't always made of the same kind or quality of wheat.

"So women used what they had, their eyes—what the dough or batter looked like—and their fingers to feel it. To be honest, I still do that to gauge the amount of flour I use for cookies and breads."

*I guess when you come right down to it, that's the way I am about a lot of things, particularly relationships—friendships. My favorite people aren't at all alike, some seeming unlikely, or a bit rough around the edges, and yet.* She removed a bit of dough from the small ball she was forming in her floured hands, then rolled it in the dish of sugar and cinnamon before placing it with others on the cookie sheet. *I can't imagine not having Rocky and Abe and Marge and Herb as friends.*

*As well as so many others!*

By the time Uncle Miltie came back in with his walker and washed at the sink, the first warm snickerdoodles were being placed on a saucer for him, the rest on the counter. He took his first bite where she could watch his enjoyment. "It's scrumptious, Gracie! As always . . . !"

She still enjoyed watching through the oven's rectangular window, seeing the cookies puff up at first, then gradually become flat again, with crinkled tops.

Her smile gradually faded as she thought of Andrew Hively's father; he must have been puffed up like that, too— appearing very big and important. But then the hot air all leaked out, leaving him in the reality of his flatness. A state in which he could not endure.

Was this true of the son, also? She could only pray— again—for him. And even more for Amy.

The phone's attachment was working fine—three telephone conversations by mid-morning, and each of the numbers was recorded. It was then the first questionable call came through. Gracie recognized the area code as a Chicago one, though the number itself was strange to her. But no one responded to her, "Hello . . . hello, who is this? . . . Is anybody there? . . . Hello?" She tried again and again, but when there was still no answer, she finally said, "All right, then, good-bye."

This was repeated within the next three or four minutes—ah, yes, three minutes and thirteen seconds, according to the recording device. She again tried to get some response on what she knew to be an open line, from the same number; she desperately wanted to connect if it was Amy—but wouldn't she answer if *she* called?

Gracie grabbed the telephone directory and looked up 773, confirming it as a greater Chicago exchange. There was no sound at all coming from the other end of the line—unless, this time, there might have been something like a heavy exhalation, perhaps a grunt—and a strange bumping sound. Or had she imagined that?

Gracie kept talking even while stretching the coiled phone wire as far as she could. She banged on the kitchen table with the sugar bowl to get Uncle Miltie's attention in the other room and he looked around, startled. Seeing her frantic beckoning, he used the remote control to shut off the TV, got to his feet and hurried as fast as possible, mouthing the question, "Amy?"

She was saying, "Perhaps you can't talk, but if this is you, Amy, please let me know. If it is, please make a noise—any sound will do, but just make it once for a *yes*, or twice for *no*."

They waited for what seemed a long time before there was

one small, weak thump of some sort—and Gracie couldn't know for sure if that was an answer. In the meantime, she was indicating to Uncle Miltie the number showing clearly there on the device he'd just installed, as she was writing on the phone pad, "Use cell phone to call Herb at police station—or home. Chicago number. Will try to keep on phone." She then carefully wrote the entire number before scrawling in big letters, *HURRY!!!*

She kept asking questions, but only occasionally got that same dull thump, done just once. "Amy," she finally said, "this time, if your answer is 'yes' please give two of those sounds, okay?"

Everything was quiet.

"Amy, are you still there?" *Oh, God, please don't let me have lost her—please, PLEASE, Lord. . . .* Gracie felt almost sick to her stomach. *Help me to be calm. Don't let me panic her!* "Amy, dear, I've talked with your parents, and they are very worried about you. You are in Chicago, aren't you?"

She waited for what seemed forever before she heard a small bumping sound. *Only one?* But then there was another, fainter still.

*YES! She answered me.* "Are you restricted somehow? Perhaps tied?"

BUMP—a very small sound, then an even tinier one.

"Are you well, and . . . ?" She'd almost asked if she was injured or in pain, but, if she were somehow restricted, or gagged, she could very well be in discomfort merely from that. Before Gracie could decide how to fix that question, make it into one Amy could answer, giving more information, she heard a different sound, perhaps someone opening a door.

And the line went dead!

Uncle Miltie was coming back into the kitchen from the other room, stage-whispering, "Herb's calling Chicago right away, then he's coming here. . . ." He stopped short, staring at her, then pushed his walker faster. "Gracie, are you all right?"

She stared at the silent phone in her left hand. "I lost her — I had Amy on the line and I *lost* her . . . !"

"Sit down, Gracie!" He was dragging a kitchen chair in her direction. "Sit down now."

She did as he said, too numb to argue or to even answer his questions. *I had Amy on the phone—I'm sure I did. But I lost her. I couldn't keep Amy on the line . and if that was, indeed, a door opening and Andrew was coming in and found her on the phone. . . .*

*Oh, God, dear Lord, help Amy!*

She knew Uncle Miltie was upset, that he was trying to help her, but he and this house and the whole world made no sense right then. He stayed there right beside her, pushing his walker to the side so he could pull her to him, his arms around her, holding her close, her head against his chest. "Gracie, dear, you did your best. . . ."

"It—wasn't enough. She *needs* me, needs *help*. . . ."

"We have no way of knowing, here where we are, but

maybe, Gracie, your talking to her might have given her even a little more courage, a little more hope. . . ."

She'd begun to shake, and there were tears starting down her cheeks, wetting the front of his shirt. *Where are you, God, when Amy needs You so? I can't see You anywhere in this mess, in spite of that anthem.*

*I know You must be—I do know You're out there, but—but please help me to see Thee, Lord! And—even more than that, be with Amy in a special way so she knows she has Someone on her side. That You are with her.*

# Nine

IF THE RED HAND OF THE CLOCK had not been going around so visibly, Gracie might not have believed that only a few minutes had passed before Herb got there. He didn't knock this time, just walked in when seeing them in the kitchen. "Any news?"

"I had her on the line, Herb—I'm sure that's who it was, but I lost her"

"How long ago?"

Uncle Miltie answered, "While you and I were on the phone."

"I tried so hard...." She couldn't get over the enormity of her failure. "The only facts I got for sure were that she is in Chicago and she's restricted in some way.

"Oh, Herb! She was trying.... I know she was!"

"So were you, Gracie." He came to stand right in front of her, looking down at her.

"I wanted to find out if she was hurt, if she was in pain—

but she didn't let me know. And I don't know why she called me instead of her family, but there must be some reason."

He looked at the numbers of the recorded calls, then fiddled with some buttons on the apparatus. "I've adjusted it to make it record all calls for playback, and to let us all hear."

"Never read instructions unless you're stumped!" Uncle Miltie was chagrined, and let them know why. "I used to get so provoked with workers who tackled anything new that way, yet here I did the same thing!"

She squeezed his hand. "As it turned out, there would have been nothing to record." *At least I don't think those "thumps" or "bumps" would have given any clues, but what do I know?*

"I've made contact with Chicago," Herb now told them. "They could even be at that address by now, if there happened to be a patrol car nearby—and if the call wasn't from a cell phone."

"I doubt that it was. I suspect she was having trouble even pushing buttons to get through to me. But what scares me most is that the last thing I heard sounded like a door opening."

The phone rang.

Herb looked at the local numbers on the display as he picked up the phone and handed it to her. "Hello?"

"Hi, Gracie. Is everything okay over there?" It was Marge. "I saw Herb come, and he looked as if he was hurrying, as though something might be wrong—"

Gracie swallowed the retort that first came into her mind—she knew Marge was genuinely concerned, not just being a busybody. "We're expecting a call, Marge—hoping to receive some information. We thought perhaps this was it."

"Oh. Well—then I guess I'd better hang up. I'll talk to you later."

Her words had come through clearly, crisply, for all of them to hear, so they now knew Herb's adjustment of that part of the new device worked also. "Thank goodness she understood the importance of our waiting for a call," Uncle Miltie exclaimed. "That woman can run on longer than any-one in the world!"

"But you know she's good-hearted," Gracie reminded him. "I'd be concerned, too, and curious, if I saw Herb hurrying up to her house."

"But you wouldn't nose into her business by calling her about it before the screen door barely shut behind him."

Still they waited, hardly tasting the fresh snickerdoodles and coffee. They talked about Marybeth, Herb's wife, who'd taught second grade during the first several years of their marriage, was now a stay-at-home mother but, he told them, was considering the possibility of returning to work next year when their youngest would be in first grade.

"I admire Marybeth's priorities," she told him, "especially since a law enforcement officer's salary isn't all that great."

He nodded. "Her pay as an elementary school teacher would be more than mine—but we agree that these first years are so very important. Believe me, the price many families, even in our own community, pay for spending too little time with their kids is far higher, in many ways, than what their extra income ever brought in!"

They also talked about the choir. "I'm pleased that Marybeth started singing with us this last year."

"Me, too, Gracie. Since I'm the one to make up staff schedules, I can usually arrange to be home on Wednesday evenings, since she enjoys it so!"

"She has such a sweet, clear soprano voice, but we can't persuade her to sing a solo, no matter how *small* a part it would be."

He reached out his mug for the refill of coffee she was offering. "I love her voice too but, well, you know that when people speak of a church's "war department," it's all too often the choir they're referring to.

"This way," he went on, "being just a member, we feel more comfortable—that there's less chance of becoming involved in the . . . shall we say, personality conflicts?"

Gracie herself had gone down that same path—but that wasn't the only reason she hadn't wanted to be considered for solo parts. In the first place, she wasn't certain she'd be good at it and, secondly, she was most satisfied listening to the others. "When you consider the range of human types, social positions, and musical talents we have there, it's a wonder things are as calm as they are."

He tilted his chair back on its rear legs and grinned at her.

"And you were thinking that during the middle of this week, right?"

Uncle Miltie responded to that teasing. "I was here. I know she was shook-up."

They were trying hard to pass the time, but there was still no call. When Uncle Miltie invited Herb to come outside and see the chrysanthemums, the younger man at first demurred, then changed his mind when the other assured him, "This is a fairly good-sized lot, but you'll easily hear the phone from any part of it."

Gracie was relieved they were gone; keeping a conversation going under these circumstances had been more difficult than she'd have expected. *I know, El, you used to kid me about never running out of things to talk about, but filling up time for the sake of just filling it is not as easy as it may seem!*

The phone finally rang—and yes, it was a Chicago number. She didn't pick it up until the beginning of the fourth ring, wanting to give Herb the chance to at least start for the house. "Hello?"

"Is this Ms. Parks?"

It was an unfamiliar male voice. "Yes, it is. And to whom am I speaking?"

"Officer Mark Jameson, calling from Chicago. May I please speak with Chief Bower?"

"One moment please." She was only slightly surprised to see that her hand was shaking as she laid down the phone. She wanted more than anything to ask how Amy was, to demand information—but she'd follow the rules as she saw them.

She hurried toward the door. "Herb, the phone—it's for you."

He was already coming in. "The one we've been waiting for?"

She nodded. "It's an officer, from Chicago."

He grabbed her hand, giving a small tug, which she took as his reassurance that it was all right for her to listen in on the conversation. She followed him, standing there in the kitchen holding on tight to the back of a wooden chair.

"This is Herb Bower."

"Mark Jameson here. I'm sorry it took so long to get back to you, but we've been very busy."

"Is Amy all right?" The crucial question.

Time seemed to freeze before the answer came, with Gracie holding her breath for what seemed *too* long, as if she were underwater and struggling for the surface. Officer Jameson's inflections remained the same, "As far as we know, there was no major physical assault, but she's been through a lot. Right now we're in the emergency room...."

*The emergency room!*

". . . They've just taken her inside to check her over, to make sure. We'll know soon, but thought you'd want to have this much, anyway."

"What condition was she in?"

"The perpetrator must have a real thing about duct tape—

it was around both knees and ankles, and around her wrists, binding them together, her arms behind her back. And not only covering her mouth, but going all the way around her head."

*Oh, Amy! How did you ever manage to call me?* But that wasn't nearly as important to Gracie right now as, "Ask if we can talk with her."

Her stage-whisper had evidently been loud enough so that the Chicago policeman said, "Tell Ms. Parks that would be fine with us, but Amy Cantrell has so far refused to speak with anyone."

She reached for the phone, which Herb relinquished readily. "Is she capable of speaking?"

"Physically, she is, as far as we know—but she acts scared to death, and won't say anything."

"Could you please tell her I really would like to speak with her? That it's important." But why should the officer trust her? "I'll make every effort to not say or do anything that could make matters worse."

"The doctors are with her right now, but I'll try that as soon as . . . hold on a minute, one's coming out. Doctor . . . Doctor Davison, may I speak with you? I'm on the phone with people from Willow Bend, Indiana, Amy Cantrell's hometown. Would it be possible for a special friend to speak with her?"

"She won't talk to anyone!"

That sounded like irritation, but could be something else she didn't even try to identify. "This is Gracie Parks. I'm the one she tried to call from—from wherever she was when the officers found her."

"That would have been impossible, Ms. Parks. . . ."

"But it *wasn't* impossible. She *did* try."

Herb's head was near hers as he verified that, "Amy did attempt to communicate with Gracie. All she got was bumping sounds or grunts—but she did the best she could."

"Well . . . we can let you try—if she's agreeable to that, but just for a moment."

Gracie endured another wait in the almost-silence of faded, indistinguishable words and activities. And then the first voice, that of the city policeman, became louder and was speaking to Gracie, "I think she understood when I asked her, though at first she just lay there."

"Is she that sick—or hurt?"

"Not as far as we know, though we don't have reports back from the lab to compare with those your Indiana hospital is faxing here. It's more like she closes her eyes—and shuts out the world." He cleared his throat. "However, she did give a little nod when I asked if you could speak to her, so just hold on a few seconds."

She pulled a chair closer to the phone, and sat down as the voice said, "Here, you hold the phone, Amy. It's your friend, Gracie."

Amy said nothing, so Gracie did. "Hi, Amy, how are you feeling?"

No answer. "I'm pleased that you called earlier, but we did seem to have difficulties, didn't we?"

*I'm not getting through to her at all!* "Were you hurt, dear? Did he do anything to hurt you?" *Please give me wisdom, God, something to latch on to so I can get through to her!* "We miss you, dear, and your beautiful voice. I'm sure you'd like to know that our choir—your choir won first place in the contest. Everyone did a good job, they did everything just right. You would have been so happy, along with us!

"And now I'm hoping you'll be coming back soon, so you can sing with us for the district competition. . . ."

She waited, then, still getting no reply, heard herself asking, "And Andrew, where is he?"

There was a gasp. "They—killed him."

"They . . . ?" She couldn't even repeat that next word, just looked at Herb, who reached for the phone.

"This is Herb Bower, Amy. Are you sure someone killed him?"

"They killed him," the weak voice repeated. "Like my father did his."

"But your dad did *not* kill his father." Though that one word was somewhat emphasized, he had spoken softly.

"Andrew told me. That's why. . . ."

He tried to get her to continue, "That's why *what?*"

"Had to show how it hurts. Now he's dead—too."

Gracie felt she should help somehow. *But what can I say,*

*God? Is Andrew really dead? What happened?* Herb had offered her the phone again, so, "Where *is* Andrew, Amy?"

"Took away. In the other ambulance." Still that slow, almost emotionless voice.

Gracie had a million questions, which she didn't feel she could ask: How had Andrew found her? How did he make friends with her? What sort of lies had he told her? How had she managed to use the telephone when her wrists were taped behind her back?

"Amy, dear, I'm going to ask a favor: please talk to the officers. Tell them exactly what happened, and why."

No response, so she tried again, this time already knowing the answer, "Are you there, Amy?"

"Um-hmmm."

"Okay, will you tell *me* about it?"

No agreement—but no discernible negative response, either. "Did he say you were going to Chicago when you left the hospital?"

"Just drove."

"Were you afraid?"

"Didn't want to come here, or go home. My father *killed* his."

Gracie looked at Herb, who was shaking his head, and mouthing, *That's not true.* "How did he prove that to you?"

"Told me. Showed the papers."

*Logic will probably not work here.*

"My father framed his—changed records. Shot him before proved innocent."

Herb was again shaking his head, so Gracie figured everything he'd checked out supported Roy's story. But Amy was convinced, and wouldn't be able to accept the truth without proof. "Are you in love with Andrew?" She couldn't help herself, now that she had Amy speaking to her.

There was a lengthy silence before, "I thought so."

*Thank You, God, that she used the past tense!* "What did Andrew do to you?"

There was again no answer. Wondering if someone else could do better, Gracie held the phone out a little, toward Herb. He raised his brows and shook his head, whispering in a very low voice, "Stay with it——if they want you to stop, they'll interrupt."

*Maybe it is I who wants to stop, because I'm not accomplishing much.* "Why did you leave the hospital, Amy?"

"Couldn't go home—Daddy killed a man."

*At least she's now referring to him as "Daddy."* "Was Andrew going to marry you?"

"Said so. . . ."

*I don't even know if Illinois requires a parent's signature for the marriage of seventeen-year-olds.* "Amy, did you see Andrew after school, before coming to the church the night you got sick?"

That little sucked-in breath again. "He didn't hurt me."

*That's too quick a defense!* "Did he give you something to eat or drink?"

"He brought me—no, NO! He *didn't* make me sick! He loves me!"

"But today he tied you up with duct tape," she reminded in as gentle a voice as she could manage.

"Wanted to go back—Indiana. He tried to change mind, but—ran away.

"Dragged back in room—grabbed phone. That's when used tape. Had to get food and—couldn't trust me. . . ." The next words were the most forceful, "Was *my* fault."

*Did he keep telling you that all the while he was applying that tape? You must have believed what he said that time, too. I'm going to have to tell you the truth.* "The reason you didn't hear of Andrew all these years, dear, is because he's been in a mental institution. . . ."

"*Not* crazy. He's not!"

"The tests they gave. . . ."

"No! *My* fault—it's mine! *Mine.* . . ." There was a high-pitched, drawn-out scream, and a loud crash followed by a rush of indistinguishable, excited voices and . . . sobbing?

Herb took the phone from her hand, and in moments was speaking to someone else. When he put it down, it was to tell Gracie that Andrew was very much alive, although he had been shot in the right shoulder—while using Amy as his shield.

The Chicago news was sobering, but the important thing was that Amy was safe now—and the authorities were notifying her family, so the Cantrells could probably be with her soon.

Gracie fretted, "What do you suppose those papers were, Herb, that Amy said Andrew showed her to 'prove' her father killed Tony Hively?" She couldn't help reverting to her sleuthing mode, especially with so much surprising information to digest.

"Perhaps Roy could have written some sort of a threat, or something," he suggested. "But that seems unlikely since Tony was on vacation when the authorities were called in."

"But—Amy referred to *the* papers. Doesn't that sound more like newspapers or documents, rather than a letter or note." She was now pacing the kitchen while trying to figure it out. "He didn't go to trial, did he?"

Herb leaned back against the refrigerator, "Not in the sense of being there in body, but there was, of course, a thorough investigation that was covered by the papers. Andrew certainly would not have shown those to her."

"That place where he stayed while in Willow Bend, did he take everything with him?"

"We'll find out." He punched in a number that was answered immediately. "Hi, Celia. Things fairly quiet there?"

*He's calling the police station and Celia Pelton is giving him information about a number of calls, and of people in to see him.*

Herb listened intently, made a few notes in the book he pulled from his shirt pocket, asked a few questions, gave some responses, then put down the phone.

"I'm heading over to where Andrew stayed. You know the place—Cordelia Fountain's home. There's always a chance that Andrew left something that can shed light on this."

Without asking permission, Gracie followed him out the door and got into his car. She herself wouldn't have even thought about the necessity of a policeman having to stop at the magistrate's office to get a search warrant before going on to the big brick house on Main Street. A small sign on its front porch read, "Rooms for Rent," and Cordelia Fountain, the seventy-ish woman who owned this old-fashioned tourist home, was soon greeting them.

"No, that nice, quiet young Mr. Hively hasn't checked out, but he left a day or two ago, taking only a small suitcase or carry-on or whatever-you-call-it." And when Herb questioned further, she told them, "As far as I know, most of his things are still in his room."

She was troubled about taking them upstairs, and remembered only after being on the third step that she might need her master key to let them in. It turned out that Andrew rented by the month, instead of by the night or week, and had come and gone a number of times during the last two or three months. No, he never told her when he'd be back, and she'd thought nothing of it when he'd departed this time.

They stopped just inside the doorway and looked around. There were two windows in this corner room, one facing the street, and the other overlooking Blackberry Alley. The furnishings were comfortably older, sort of like their aproned owner, making Gracie feel at ease. A laptop computer was on the table directly across the room, and a number of papers and manilla folders were both there and on the four-poster bed.

Cordelia was worried about them going through her renter's things. Herb showed her the search warrant—but that made her even more uneasy. "Does that mean he's a *criminal* or something?"

Once she'd begun fretting, she wasn't much calmed by Herb's saying he didn't think she had to worry about that, and his pointing out that he was taking full responsibility for their being there. She was clearly hesitant about leaving them in the room when her phone rang.

"I'm too much like that, too," Gracie admitted. "I always have to answer my phone when I hear it. But it's a good thing for her sake and ours that she left when she did."

He nodded, but said nothing as he continued quickly going through the folders, page-by-page. She was doing the same with the ones on the bed, then got down on her knees to check beneath it. Pulling out a large suitcase, she was surprised to find it unlocked.

Inside were underclothes, several shirts, socks, and a pair of sweatpants. Lifting these items out, however, Gracie saw a small pile of what looked like fairly expensive paper. "Herb?" He looked around, eyebrows raised in question. "Come see this."

There were three copies of almost the same thing, in each only a word or two changed. It was a hand-printed apology for ruining someone's life—with no salutation nor signature on any of them.

"Was he—practicing?" she wondered. "Maybe something to show Amy, saying it was from her father?

"Possibly." His lips were straight across, pressed together. "Whichever one—or a different one—he showed her was probably all the 'proof' this unsophisticated seventeen-year-old needed." They searched the rest of the room, but found nothing else they considered suspicious. Gracie, however, realized she could be looking straight at some crucial clue and not realize its significance.

From the police station, where she'd returned with Herb, she called home: Everything there was under control, according to Uncle Miltie, so they could no longer put off going to the Cantrells' house.

Linda looked haggard, as though she hadn't slept for a week, but invited them inside, reminding them that Roy was at work. "He's never here at this time—though it shouldn't be long now. I just got a call from the authorities in Chicago and—and I phoned for Roy to come home right away. They'll talk to both of us then. . . ."

Gracie nodded. "And we wanted to tell you that we did get to talk to Amy."

"You did?" Wide-eyed, she stared at them. "Why didn't they let me talk to her then? Is she all right?"

"Herb and I both. . . ."

"What's she doing in Chicago?"

"I'm not sure why, but that's where Andrew took her."

"*Andrew*." Fear, contempt, and hatred were wrapped up in that one word. "That awful, beastly man! They'll send him to jail for kidnapping her, for taking her across state lines, won't they?"

Gracie let Herb answer, who only said that it was for the law enforcement officers and courts to decide. Though, of course, this did not satisfy Linda. She'd jumped to the conclusion that Amy was safe, so became perturbed all over again upon finding out that her daughter had been in an emergency room when they'd spoken to her.

How badly was she hurt? Would she be admitted? When could she come home? She was sure Roy would take off work and go with her to bring Amy home.

Herb suggested that they make no definite plans right away—it was too early for that. He did give assurance that he'd get back in touch as soon as he heard anything more, but they left Linda far less than happy. Gracie sighed as they went down the walk. "I don't think I'd like your job, Herb, if it's always like this."

"This is a *good* day, Gracie," he told her. "It's when I must tell someone that a loved one is dead, or mixed-up with a gang, or overdosed and never coming home that it's really bad."

Gracie nodded. That would, indeed, be much worse— something she hoped she'd never have to experience.

# Ten

I MUST HAVE LOOKED *at that clock twenty times since get-ting back!* She'd told Uncle Miltie about the stop at the Cantrells, but when Marge showed up a little later, Gracie kept the conversation on the subject of the choir, Anna's continuing loss of sight, and a mutual friend who'd been taken to the hospital with a heart attack.

Since their neighbor didn't come right out and ask any questions about Amy or mention Herb's being there, Gracie, surprised but relieved, was not about to give her an opening. Only as she was leaving did Marge say, "Well, I hope things straighten out—and that Amy comes back soon."

"We're praying for that." Gracie closed the kitchen door behind her friend, then sagged back against it. "Well, Uncle Miltie, we got through that—though not very well, I'm afraid."

"At least we did get through it—and without stretching the truth or telling her off." He smiled crookedly. "We could have done worse."

It was after he went back into the other room that she acted upon the idea that had been tugging at her mind.

⚯

"Aunt Gracie!" It was a cry of delight over the phone lines. "How wonderful to hear from you!"

"You've been inviting me for a long time now, Carter, to visit you in Chicago, so I'm wondering if that's still a possibility."

"Of course it is! How soon can you make it?"

"What about late this afternoon—or is that too soon?"

Carter Stephens laughed. "Just about right—but something tells me you've got more in that fertile mind of yours than just making a visit to me."

"Well, now that you mention it, yes, I do," and she briefly filled her in on the situation with Amy, and with Andrew.

"Ah, so you intend to do some amateur sleuthing."

"I need to be there, to talk with Amy if I can—to try figuring out what's going on now, as well as what took place some five years ago—and this last couple of months."

"And you're hoping I can help."

This wasn't a question, and Gracie was honest enough not to respond as though it was. "I have a responsibility, dear. I'm the one she called, not her father at work or her mother at home or her pastor at church.

"And I'm the one she talked to while in that Chicago emergency room, even when she wouldn't say anything to people there. I'm not a psychologist or anything. . . ."

Carter put in dryly, "You may not be a psychologist, dear auntie, but I challenge that anything. You forget that I've seen you in action—that I know when you're out to get information."

"I'm that notorious a busybody?"

She'd let her voice sound as though her feelings were hurt, but Carter's voice showed amused love when responding, "If you used 'noted' rather than 'notorious,' and 'concerned friend' for 'busybody,' you'd have it just about right."

"Ah, these lawyers, nitpicking over getting exactly the right word! This isn't a billion-dollar lawsuit, dear, nor a capital crime—at least as far as we know." But then she had to get back to Amy's situation. "Herb has been doing a lot of checking, and seems convinced that the story as told by her parents is the truth. However, we suspect that Andrew is deluded enough to believe his own version of what happened, no matter what proof there is to the contrary.

"And Amy doesn't understand that?"

"Apparently not, so that's why I need to come right away, hopefully before her parents get there." She almost stumbled over asking, "Are there any skids you could grease for me, dear? Any way of helping your small-town aunt—not a police officer or lawyer or licensed private eye—to get to see her?"

"I'm—not sure. . . ."

"I don't want you to do anything that could get you in trouble," she hastened to add. "It's just that, being in the DA's office and knowing people. . . ."

"This isn't Willow Bend, dear."

"I'm aware of that." She sighed. "Well, so much for that idea."

There was a moment of silence before, "Why don't you come anyway, Aunt Gracie? We'll just have to see how things work out."

❦

The first thing that worked out differently took place while she was still in Willow Bend. "But I don't expect to stay long, Uncle Miltie," she told him when he stated that if she went, he was going, too. "You can stay here and take care of Gooseberry for me."

"No way, Gracie! That cat can very well take care of himself, what with that automatic watering thing and that special feeder you bought."

"But if I need to stay more than a day or two. . . ."

He finished her sentence in his own way. ". . . Then Miss Inquisitive next door can come over and refill both containers."

He'd gotten to his feet to face her, as though that gave him more authority than sitting there in his recliner, and it suddenly struck her as funny. "You always have an answer, don't you?"

He grinned at her, obviously realizing she was weakening. "Only when I'm right."

"Which you always think you are!" But she was laughing as she reentered the kitchen, calling back from there, "I'm leaving in about an hour—at the very latest."

"And I'll be sitting there right beside you," he called back, heading for his bedroom, off the living room. "Carter's my grand-niece and I haven't seen her for far too long a time."

They did meet her timetable, walking out together after she'd already transported their two suitcases and two "care packages," as he called them: sturdy plastic containers of chocolate cookies from the freezer and of snickerdoodles. They made excellent time and, earlier than expected, got to the waiting room on Carter's floor, in the department of the District Attorney.

Gracie's niece was a graceful, blonde, attractive five-nine, with legs and ankles still as slender and shapely in those flat pumps as they'd been ten years earlier when she graduated from high school. She crossed the room to meet them. "It's so good to see you," she exclaimed happily, reaching out for her aunt.

Gracie embraced her. "It's been much too long, dear."

And Uncle Miltie pushed his walker to the side so he could take her into his arms. "Carter! You look great—and feel that way, too."

"So do you—both of you." But then she turned toward the three men in the room and made introductions.

The oldest, Jim Riley, smiled pleasantly as he shook Gracie's hand. "Carter's been filling us in about you."

"Uh-oh! That doesn't sound good at all." She tried to sound and look worried. "That's why all four of you are here to greet us, right?"

"Only in one sense." He laughed. "We think a lot of this

young woman, and any relatives of hers are welcome here."

It was on the tip of Gracie's tongue to say they could prove their welcome by helping with the Amy problem, but was extra glad she hadn't uttered anything that flippant when he added, "We've even helped her find some information for you."

Carter nodded as Gracie looked toward her, but spoke to the others. "And it's now time for you guys to get back to work covering for me as I take my aunt and uncle into my office."

"Slave driver!" Jim grumbled, but there was a twinkle in his eye as he looked back at Gracie—and winked.

Once inside, Carter sat down in her wheeled office chair as Gracie and Milton settled themselves across from her. "I'd planned to spend some time visiting before getting into Amy's situation, but since my big-mouthed friend and co-worker jumped the gun, I'll fill you in on what we've determined thus far."

Andrew had maintained a small apartment locally for over a year, despite his history, landing a job at one of the area's country clubs as a companion or special caddie or something for some of the best golfers—and as golfing coach for advanced adults and older teens.

She'd learned nothing there of a negative nature, with the possible exception of his never having socialized much with other employees. He'd insisted on having two days off each week, scheduled at least seven days ahead, though not necessarily the same ones. He had proved unreachable on those days, for members of the staff had tried on a number of occasions to contact him.

"That must be when he went to see Amy," Gracie murmured, then sat back in her chair and resolved to just listen when Carter nodded and went on with facts. There were few phone calls on record, but he did keep in touch, though sporadically, with his mother, who still lives in Florida, and occasionally spoke with his sister, who's married to a doctor in Paris. He appears to have no close friends, but did spend some evenings in a bar not far from where he lived.

Uncle Miltie asked if anyone had implied that he'd been acting crazy or strange. Carter shrugged. "Some thought so, but let's face it, if an official came to—well, to your neighbor Marge, for example, asking questions about someone she knows in Willow Bend, isn't it probable she'd find the situation odd enough to make her think the person being discussed was, in fact, a bit strange?"

He frowned. "I can't really picture many folks reacting that way, Carter, but yeah, the one you mentioned just might."

Gracie would have liked to defend her friend, but it wasn't the right time, so she left Uncle Miltie's comment unchallenged. "What sort of professional reports did you get about him?"

"They commended his natural golfing skills and his ability to help people work at improving their own games. He obviously made the most favorable impression on the wealthy doctors, lawyers, and others he accompanied around the course—but many found him hard to figure out. As one co-worker put it, 'I feel I know Andrew less well today than I thought I did the day we met.'"

"What does he himself have to say about bringing Amy to his apartment—and confining her the way he did?"

"Nothing."

"*Nothing*?"

"Not about that. His having been shot in the right shoulder has him terribly upset; he fears he'll never play golf again—or not as well."

Uncle Miltie sat there shaking his head. "And that's apparently the one thing at which he excels."

"Or did, Uncle Miltie," Carter corrected. "And he places all the blame for that on the police."

"Is surgery required?"

"They've already removed the bullet and taken out some bone fragments—and predict he'll be fine, given time and therapy."

"Have you talked with him, Carter?"

She shook her head. "No. The person who did just got silence most of the time, and hatred—abhorrence, actually, for anything connected with law enforcement."

Gracie was desperate to learn more about her young friend. "Is there anything new concerning Amy? Is she talking about having been brought here—and other things?"

"Very little. Even when told that her parents were on the

way, she just rolled over on her side, facing the wall, and pulled the covers over her head."

"I presume that this hospital's been notified about her disappearance from ours . . . ?"

"Of course."

"And with Andrew?"

Carter's eyes flashed. "He's not going anywhere."

Gracie let out a sigh of relief; she'd feared a possible repeat of what had so recently taken place. "When can I see Amy?"

There was a slight pause before, "You're not going to like this. . . ."

"I *can't* see her after coming all this way?" Gracie tried to hide her disappointment.

A slight smile. "There's only one condition."

"Which is?"

"Well, it's two, really. We'd like you to pay close attention to everything she tells you—but the guard must remain in the room with you."

"Oh, Carter! I'm afraid she won't talk if there's anyone else there!"

"You're our major hope right now for getting anything out of her, and that's extremely important as to our helping her— as well as to determining what to do as far as Andrew's concerned. Besides, once her parents arrive, they'll certainly want her to rest rather than answer our questions."

"At this moment," Uncle Miltie put in, voice and manner stony, "I don't have much concern for that young man."

"I understand your feelings, but at this point the only thing we have on him legally is his use of that duct tape. As you recall, it was Amy who called him from the hospital, and she sneaked out of there to be with him.

"We have no proof that she objected to leaving home and coming to Chicago."

Uncle Miltie leaned forward, arms on his walker. "He certainly wouldn't have had to keep her there by using all that duct tape if she *wanted* to be with him."

"That seems logical to you and me, but his lawyer could come up with any number of possibilities to be considered— like her trying to kill herself or their having a lovers quarrel or ever her threatening to kill him."

"Carter!"

"By the time a defense lawyer presented Andrew's side of the story, with whatever asides or embellishments were considered necessary, at least some on the jury wouldn't be sure he'd done anything more than he had to in order to protect *her*."

At the hospital Gracie found she had been cleared by both the legal and medical authorities. She had no worries that Uncle Miltie would want to go upstairs to Amy's room with her, but was nonetheless relieved when he assured her, "I'll wait down here in the lobby for however long it takes."

"Thank you," she said, and meant it.

He was looking through the *Guideposts* magazine on one of

the tables as she got on the elevator. It was a short ride, but the only time since her shower and getting dressed this morning in which Gracie had been alone.

*Dear Lord, please give me the words to say and the wisdom to tell the difference between what might be my own thoughts and what You're giving me. And please make her receptive to what I'm saying, and willing to share. And, oh, yes, do help me to remember—exactly!—any truly important parts of whatever I may learn.*

The doors opened, and she drew in a deep breath before stepping out and approaching the nursing station. An older woman wearing an oblong white pin indicating she was a volunteer came to the counter, smiling, and Gracie introduced herself with, "I'm Grace Parks, and have come to see Amy Cantrell."

A look of caution came over the attractive face. "I'm sorry, Ms. Parks, but Miss Cantrell isn't. . . ."

"It's all right, Marie. Mrs. Parks has permission to go to her." A middle-aged nurse had overheard, and came to place a hand on the arm of the volunteer for a moment before leading Gracie back down the corridor. Just as they reached the room at the end of the hall, however, she paused to ask almost apologetically, "Just for my records, Mrs. Parks, may I see some photo identification?"

"Of course." Gracie reached into her large purse—and almost gasped as her fingers touched the small tape recorder she'd forgotten to remove following Sunday morning's taping of the run-through of *Help Me to See Thee, Lord!* Even as she was pulling out her wallet and flipping it open to show her driver's license, she was silently thanking God, *So this is how You arranged for information to be retained exactly.*

"Surprise, Amy," the nurse greeted as they entered together. "Look who's come to see you."

Amy had been lying flat on her back, staring up at the ceiling, and for that first moment looked pleased. But then her gaze flicked from Gracie toward the blue-uniformed woman sitting between the bed and door and she seemed to—to what? To freeze in place, like that tag-game Gracie and her young childhood friends used to play.

Gracie paid little attention to the nurse's almost inaudible murmur to the guard that this was the woman who'd been okayed by both the police and Amy's doctor. She bent over the bed to give Amy a hug and to kiss her. "I've been really worried about you, dear."

The girl's arms had started to rise, as though to return the embrace, then dropped down again on the bed; her eyes shifted just enough to almost meet Gracie's, but not quite. "I know."

*That acknowledgment's at least a start.* "Are you feeling better now, Amy?" Gracie had already made the decision not to upset Amy by mentioning her parents.

As the silence grew longer, it was all Gracie could do to keep from rushing on to another question. The room seemed loud with silence, faraway indistinguishable voices only emphasizing the lack of words here.

*Be still, and know.* The words were as clear in her head as though Amy had spoken them, and they calmed Gracie's nervousness. Then Amy said, in what was no more than a raspy whisper, "I'm s-o-o-o tired."

As Gracie's one hand moved along Amy's forearm, trying to soothe with her touch as well as keeping her voice as soft as her young friend's, her other hand slipped back inside her purse to press that ON button. She also walked around the bed, to be on the window side of the room so Amy might not be as conscious of the guard's presence. "You've been through so much, dear. It's bound to have taken a lot out of you."

The barest hint of a nod. "He said he loved me."

"And you loved him, too." She must have, to come with him to Chicago.

"I did."

*Good—she used the past tense!* "Andrew is going to be all right, Amy."

Her eyelids closed and Gracie was sure that the strain on her face was an indication of the girl's dealing with intense pain. "They shot him—he fell down on the floor and they carried him away." Her head moved from one side to the other, tears forming. "Andrew is dead. . . ."

"No, dear. Andrew is very much alive."

"Have you *seen* him?"

"No, but. . . ."

"You believe *those* people, the ones who were out to get him."

Gracie was about to deny that, but there was that persistent little voice again: *Be still....* She argued inwardly that this was the time to make Amy realize the truth, but.... *Okay, God, I'll try to do it Your way—even if it doesn't seem to make sense.*

Perhaps the silence was making Amy edgy, for she shifted position. "I didn't want it to be secret, but it was too dangerous."

"Dangerous for whom, dear?"

"For Andrew. People were after him, people from before, whom my father knew—they all wanted him dead.

"Daddy, too." Tears were flowing from the outer corners of her eyes, down to her ears, and Gracie tried to blot them with tissues from the box on the bedside table.

"It's *my* fault." Amy's voice was a bare whimper. "I shouldn't have tried to run away, I shouldn't have tried to call you, but I—was so scared."

Gracie wanted to reassure her that she'd done nothing wrong, that she'd had every reason to be scared. "What did Andrew say he was going to do after you got to Chicago?"

"We wanted to get married."

"What did he want to do before getting married?" *I hope, God, that I'm asking some of the right things—at least she's giving answers. Don't let me bungle this!*

"I—don't know."

"You said he had to leave you for a while. What did you think he was going to do when he left?"

Amy shut her eyes again. "He said he must get food. . . ."

Gracie tried again. "Was this his usual apartment—where he lived most of the time?" *I didn't even realize I had that question in mind!* "Or did he take you somewhere else?"

She looked puzzled. "I—assumed it was where he lived but—there was no food, not even crackers, or cans of vegetables—or milk. Not anything. . . . And I was so hungry."

She finally said, managing only a whisper. "Why did he take me?"

*At least she's finally beginning to question his actions, his motives!* "What was the apartment like?"

"Old. Dirty. Small. He said it was just for now, that he'd rented it furnished, saving money so we could look, together, for the one we wanted."

*The phone was already there, or the police couldn't have found her—even if it hardly seemed like a home.* "How was it laid out? How many rooms were there?" *I never asked Carter that.*

"One room. And small bath. A tiny kitchenette in one corner—and the couch pulled out to make a queen-sized bed. I said we shouldn't—sleep together before we got married and—and he laughed, and said we'd work something out. But he did put a blanket on the floor to sleep last night.

"He put it right in front of the door, so I wonder, now, if, even then, he didn't trust me to stay."

There was another pause before, "He locked the door and took the key when he left this morning, saying he was going for food."

Again a lengthy silence, as she moved restlessly on the high hospital bed. "I got—scared. I didn't *want* to be locked in, and I was so hungry. The phone was working, but I couldn't call home." The words had become a wail, like those of a child. "Not after leaving like that, and besides, Daddy . . ." Her head turned from side to side on the pillow. "I knew if I did, they'd do something *awful* to Andrew."

Gracie continued to stroke the girl's arm. She was relieved to know that the guard was writing something over there, and wondered if any of this was getting recorded on the tape hidden in her purse.

Amy went on, "I remembered your number and—and your helping on Friday night, and staying at the hospital, and coming to see me."

Amy again looked straight up at the acoustic-tile ceiling. "I didn't expect he'd come back so soon, to check on me! I should have waited longer before trying to use the phone, because when he came in and saw what I was doing he—he was furious—not just mad, but disappointed in me, and hurt. He said he'd thought I loved him but saw now that, like everyone else, I had turned against him.

"That's when he got the duct tape from a drawer, and started to use it, first fastening my wrists behind me, then covering my mouth when I started to beg him not to. . . ."

Gracie was almost overwhelmed by bone-deep sorrow. "And you let him do it to you. . . ."

"I *had* to. So many in his life had proved unfaithful, especially my own father—and here I was, too, having been proved untrustworthy.

"Don't you see? I couldn't let him be hurt anymore."

Gracie looked at those youthfully rounded cheeks still red-dened and splotchy from the removal of the duct tape. "And then you called me."

She nodded. "He left again, and the longer I lay there on the floor the more terrified I got. It seemed like hours—though I now know that it wasn't—I thought he'd been so upset with me that maybe he wouldn't ever come back.

"So—I tried banging my feet on the floor, but he'd taken my shoes off—and then I rolled over and over to get to the door, but nobody came when I kicked against that, either."

Reliving the experience was traumatic, but Gracie had to let her go on. "I figured I had to try something else, so flopped myself back close to the table and—and finally man-aged to get up on my feet—then sort of inched sideways till I could lean against the table, where the phone was. But I still had an awful time trying to get the right buttons with my wrists fastened together behind me."

*Your poor wrists, too, are cut and bruised! They must be very painful.*

"Then, just when I tried for that last digit, the phone fell off the table. So I had to get *back* down on the floor, and get it shut off so I could start over."

"But you did get me, dear. You got through to me, but I couldn't get a response from you."

"I—couldn't hear you, not till there at the very end, after I'd tried and tried and *tried*. And by then I was crying, and my nose was running, and I was so terribly afraid!"

*Thank You, God, for making her keep trying—and for our finding out the number—and for getting word to the authorities in time....* "You did very well, Amy, with your bumping noises, your answering my questions."

"I had to sort of bang the phone to do that—and I think I messed it up...."

"You did fine!"

"Then Andrew came! And he—he was so angry, and I got even more scared, for I'd never seen him like that. He—finally calmed down enough to make a sandwich for himself—cold meat in a roll. But I couldn't have any of that, or even water, because he couldn't trust me not to yell or scream or anything if he took the tape off."

"He *loved* me...." It was a cry of agony, of loss, and Gracie stayed with her, holding her close for the time it took to work through what had happened. She also attempted to explain to Amy why her parents had kept from her the extent of the problems in Florida—that they'd wanted her to have a more normal childhood in Indiana than they'd felt she could have if they had stayed where they were.

It was then that Gracie was asked to come to the lounge.

# Eleven

LINDA AND ROY HAD ARRIVED shortly after Gracie did—but weren't "cleared" to see their daughter until after meeting with the police and one of the doctors, who finally sent the nurse to request Gracie to join them.

She shared with them what she considered the most important parts of her lengthy conversation with Amy, saying she felt the girl was at least beginning to understand not only her parents' situation, but also the mental state of Andrew. "I doubt, however, that she even yet comprehends the danger she was in—and she still feels guilty about not helping Andrew more."

Carter accepted from Gracie the recording, which they hoped would cover much of the early part of her talk with Amy, holding it as carefully as though it were a most fragile piece of antique glass. "At least this is a start."

"Does she have to know right away about my taping our

conversation?" Gracie asked. "I don't want her feeling betrayed by me, too."

Jim and the Cantrells assured her this would be avoided if at all possible so, after going back in to say good-bye to Amy, Gracie felt comfortable leaving with Carter and Uncle Miltie.

"You are staying for a nice long visit, aren't you?" Carter asked as they walked together to the parking lot.

"Probably a day or so," Uncle Miltie told her. But Gracie just said, "We'll see."

Carter laughed. "I'm not about to push my luck any further—I'm just glad you're not heading back for Willow Bend at this very moment!" She invited Uncle Miltie to ride with her to her townhouse complex while Gracie in the other car would follow. "You and Aunt Gracie get to talk to each other all the time, so I demand at least a little of your undivided attention."

He was obviously pleased, and Gracie felt relieved to be alone right then—though she wouldn't have admitted that. When she arrived at Carter's condominium, decorated somewhat sparingly but in excellent taste with mid-to-late nineteenth-century furniture, she couldn't help but compare this with her mental picture of where Amy had been taken.

Uncle Miltie insisted that they choose anywhere they wanted to go for dinner, on him—but Gracie suggested they defer that option to the following evening. "I appreciate the offer, but I'm exhausted. Speaking only for myself, I'd rather Carter would just heat up a can of soup."

"I'm sure you are tired. What a time you've had these last few days!" Their niece looked from Gracie to her uncle. "How about it? Shall we go along with her suggestion to eat here tonight?"

"To be honest, that would suit me better, too." And then, pretending to keep Gracie from hearing by tipping his open hand over his mouth, he stage-whispered, "And this way we'll know that she's going to stay at least until day after tomorrow."

"Good thinking, Uncle Miltie!" she responded in the same fashion and, laughing, headed for the kitchen.

In remarkably short order she was serving them a delicious chicken/broccoli/carrot stir-fry with rice, and her great-uncle was telling Gracie that postponing their restaurant jaunt was one of her best ideas ever.

It was after eating that Gracie asked Carter if it would be all right for her to call Herb about what took place today. "I know he'll get an official report, but I'd sort of like talking to him, if that's allowed. He's been so very concerned and. . . ." Her voice trailed off.

Carter looked thoughtful, then nodded slowly. "Ordinarily, I'd have to refuse, but it should be all right if you want to tell him just the bare bones of what took place. He'll be learning the whole story soon enough."

So Gracie did phone the station and left a message. He called back from home within a few minutes, sounding worried, "Are you all right, Gracie?"

"Very much so, Herb—and I think Amy will be, too. I had a long talk with her, and then her parents went in to see her. I don't know how they made out, but at least the ground-work was laid."

"She wasn't—hurt?"

She hesitated before replying. "Emotionally, she is—as well as psychologically. But not too much physically, thank God! Not seriously, anyway."

Then, changing the topic, he asked, "So when are you coming home?"

"I'm not sure, but—probably day after tomorrow."

Apparently realizing the question to which her aunt had responded, Carter spoke quite loudly, "But I'm going to try extending that, Herb."

Gracie grinned at her, even telling Herb, "Gooseberry will be missing me, and he's apt to run out of food or water if I'm gone too long."

"Tell ya what, Gracie," he offered, "I'll personally tell Marge that she's delegated to see that doesn't happen."

She laughed. "Never mind, Herb. Should I happen to stay an extra day, I'll gladly take on the assignment of alerting Marge."

She and Uncle Miltie prepared to leave on their second morning, at the same time as Carter. "We had a wonderful visit," she assured her niece, "and I can't possibly express how much I appreciate all you and Jim and the others did to help Amy.

Carter gave a mock curtsy—"You're welcome. You did so well that we might call on you some other time when having problems getting people to respond."

And Uncle Miltie suggested, "At the same rate of pay, right?"

She raised her brows. "Of course!"

"That's just about what it's worth—nothing!" Gracie agreed. "But I'll always be grateful for having had this opportunity."

᠕

The return trip was uneventful. As they entered the outskirts of Willow Bend, she heard the whisper of a sighed, "Home! We're home again."

She smiled across at him. He had never suggested leaving her and Willow Bend, but to know that it was truly *home* to him pleased her. "Indeed, Uncle Miltie, it's good to be home—especially now that we can be almost positive that Amy, too, will be back soon."

There were no more words exchanged—none needed. Then she caught herself humming *Hallelujah, Save Us, Lord,* which they'd sung last Sunday. *We had no idea when we got that music, God, how desperately we'd soon be calling upon You. Thanks for "saving" Amy, and for letting me be a part of that. I pray that You will continue healing her and her family, and that they will become more conscious of Your holding them in Your hand.*

But that wasn't enough, was it? *Please forgive me for not having prayed for Andrew, too, for he has obviously been miserable. And for his family, who must be every bit as heartsick about all this as Amy's. Only You can heal such long-standing pain, such misunderstanding. . . .*

They were coming down Main Street; although they'd been gone such a short time, she was noting individual stores and fire hydrants and trees. And right there was the tall, stained-glass clock on the corner of Main and Cherry Streets, the one the Lions Club and Rotary Club and Volunteer Firemen had joined in erecting in honor of all the public servants who'd given so much of their lives to Willow Bend.

Everything was clear and distinct, uniquely *home*, and she couldn't keep from smiling. She was coming down her own street, pulling into the driveway, when she happened to glance over to see Gooseberry looking out the window over the sink, raising one paw to the glass.

He wasn't supposed to be up there, but she was as eager to see him as he obviously was to see her.

To *see* one another. *We kept singing that we wanted to see You, Lord, in everything. Well, You certainly took us up on that, didn't You? Only You could have pulled this off with Amy—so that now she can get help, and so can Andrew.*

*And now that we're back, that we're home, even in the "busy-*

*ness" of our lives please help us to make the concerted effort to keep seeing You in all that's good.*

She got out of the car and helped Uncle Miltie set up his folding walker. Gooseberry was no longer in the window, but was undoubtedly waiting right inside the kitchen door. She didn't need to rush but would walk beside her uncle, who was stiff from the long ride.

He stopped halfway up the walk, looking around at the massed chrysanthemums and asters and other autumn beauties. "I'm glad there was no frost while we were gone."

She nodded, and the last two lines of their anthem suddenly came to mind:

> *Let me always choose to be*
> *With You in one accord,*
> *Then and only then will I*
> *With Your help, see Thee, Lord.*

R E C I P E

# Snickerdoodles

*(See below for changes suggested by Gracie)*

✓ 2 cups lard
✓ 3 cups sugar        } Mix real well
✓ 4 medium eggs

✓ 4 teaspoons cream of tartar
✓ 2 teaspoons soda        } Sift all these together
✓ 1 teaspoon salt
✓ Use enough flour to stiffen

Make sure dough is cool, then roll with hands into walnut-sized balls. Roll each ball in mixture of 4 teaspoons cinnamon and 4 tablespoons sugar and place two inches apart on cookie sheet (doesn't need grease).

Bake in a moderately hot oven for maybe 8 or 10 minutes—till light brown but still soft. The oven temperature I use is 375 degrees.

*(I use vegetable shortening instead of lard, and the whites of 4 extra-large eggs or of 6 medium ones instead of the 4 whole medium eggs.)

# About the Author

EILEEN M. BERGER has been writing since college, and had hundreds of stories, articles and poems published before she received a contract for her first already completed manuscript—then two more were sold within thirteen months!

Six others have followed, including her biblical novels, *The Samaritan Woman* and *The Deacon's Daughter*, also published by Guideposts. She'd had many shorter manuscripts in anthologies, from the eleven prayers in Guideposts' *Prayers for Every Need*, to stories, articles and a 20,000-word novella.

Eileen's husband Bob is still the most-loved and important person in her life, with close runners-up being their grown children: Vicki, an educator and scientist; Jim, a minister and historian; and Bill, a bridge specialist with an engineering group. Their seven wonderful grandchildren, aged from three to fifteen, are jewels in Eileen and Bob's crowns of happiness.

Though raised on a farm and living for a time both in Philadelphia, Pennsylvania, and Lansing, Michigan, she appreciates spending her married life in and near the relatively small town of Hughesville, Pennsylvania, where her husband served as pastor for many years. They continue to own and operate Berger's Choose and Cut Christmas Tree business.

Eileen understands and relates to small-town people and situations in Willow Bend, Indiana, the site of the Church Choir Mysteries series. However, although both places have churches, volunteer firefighters' organizations and county fairs, none of Eileen's real-life situations are reflected in her books, which are entirely fiction.

## A NOTE FROM THE EDITORS